Tom Fletcher
and the
Angel of Death

D0615909

Also by Sarah Matthias published by Catnip

The Riddle of the Poisoned Monk

Tom Fletcher
and the
Angel of Death

Sarah Matthias

For Lily Hutton with love

CATNIP BOOKS

Published by Catnip Publishing Ltd

14 Greville Street

London EC1N 8SB

First published in paperback 2008

1 3 5 7 9 10 8 6 4 2

Text copyright © Sarah Matthias 2008

A CIP catalogue record for this book is available from the British Library

ISBN 978-1-84647-055-4

Printed in Poland

www.catnippublishing.co.uk

Contents

Part One The Wheel of Fire

Part Two The Wheel of Fortune

Part Three The Wheel of the Year

Characters

The Novices

Tom Fletcher	chief novice – son of a local arrow maker
Herbert Glanville	novice – son of a local corn merchant
Edmund	youngest novice – orphan
Felix	a novice
Odo	a novice

The Monks

Abbot Theodore	Abbot of Saint Wilfred's Abbey
Prior Solomon	Prior of Abbey
Brother Benedict	Bursar and Keeper of the Beast House
Brother Dunstan	Novice Master

Brother Ambrose	Quill Master
Brother Fergus	Sacrist, in charge of chalices and monastery treasures including the sacred relic of Saint Wilfred's bunion.
Brother Ethelwig	Inventor and Keeper of the Bell Tower
Brother Silas	Physician

Townspeople of Saint Agnes Next-the-Sea

Job Pug	Belfry assistant
Mistress Job	his wife
Gabriel Miller	Miller
Agnes Miller	his wife
Bessie Miller	their daughter
Sir Ranulf de Lacy	Lord of Micklow Manor
Sir Percy FitzNigel	The King's Justice
Fustian	Clerk to Sir Percy
Eli Abrahams	Moneylender
Abigail Abrahams	his daughter and Bessie's best friend

Part One

The Wheel of Fire

Prologue

Human Meat

Delilah licked her yellow teeth. The boy had tasted most peculiar, but then she had not tasted human meat before. Perhaps it was always so sweet. The lioness yawned. She would like to have slept now, her stomach full and the flavours still fresh in her mouth, but there was such a commotion outside the bars of her cage, such wild crying. All those staring eyes – and the old man who looked so like the boy she had just eaten was screaming at the fat monk – the one who usually brought in the offal bucket.

"My boy! My little one!" he howled, eyes wild with pain. "My Obadiah!"

"Don't blame me, Job Pug," blustered the red faced monk, shaking the old servant roughly from his sleeve. "It's not my fault. How was I to know the handle would stick? I gave him a job, didn't I? You'll get his wages up 'til today, if that's what you're worried about!"

And then there was the woman – that was the worst of it – down on her knees at the cage, rattling the bars, arms stretched through, clawing at the air, not screaming but wailing – a terrible high pitched keening sound that hurt Delilah's ears.

But what could be amiss? After all, it was just a regular Sunday afternoon at Saint Wilfred's Abbey, the usual time that fat Brother Benedict fed his animals. The only odd thing about this afternoon was that her prey had tried to get away instead of slopping out of a pail in a quivering mass of cold flesh. Not quite as satisfying as stalking the plains of Africa, but better than staring desolately through the bars of a prison, waiting like a helpless cub to be fed.

Delilah growled nervously, a hunted look in her amber eyes, and then she flung back her broad head as a deep grumbling sound began to rise from the depths of her belly. The anguished onlookers gasped in horror as the rumble grew, rising up through her powerful shoulders, rippling the muscles of her massive neck, erupting at last from her gaping red mouth in a ferocious roar of bewilderment and fear.

Chapter 1

Fish Hooks and Conkers

Saint Wilfred's was no ordinary monastery, which was just as well, because Tom Fletcher was no ordinary novice. He certainly never intended to become a monk, as he had told his father tearfully at the headstrong age of seven, when kicking and biting, he had arrived at the great bronze doors of the abbey to be left in the care of the Brothers. But as the youngest of ten children, his desperate parents had little choice. There were simply too many hungry bellies, and Tom owned the hungriest – a surprising fact, since he was as bony a little urchin as you could ever have the ill-luck to meet.

He was also the least obedient child in the family; a detail which his anxious father kept strictly to himself, that frosty winter's day nearly six years ago, when Tom first pulled the grey woollen habit of a novice over his untidy thatch of chestnut hair and emerged the other end as Brother Thomas.

Hiding his tear stained face from the other boys, Tom pushed his meagre bundle under a lumpy mattress in the draughty novices' dormitory. It contained everything he possessed in the world – to be more precise: a fish hook, a piece of frayed string, two prize conkers and a spare pair of scratchy underpants (five sizes too big). These he generously donated to plump Herbert Glanville, the son of a local corn merchant, younger by only a few months but twice Tom's size. Herbert had dried his eyes already and was comforting himself with a greasy mutton pasty on the next hay pallet along. It was a fine beginning to a firm friendship, cemented as the years rolled round by memories of practical jokes played on those monks least likely to see the funny side of life.

Strict monastery rules about eating very little, and doing exactly what you were told, would have proved impossible for a high spirited boy like Tom, but in this he was fortunate. For their leader, Abbot Theodore, was a worldly man – an old soldier, who had lost an eye in the Crusades. And under his easy-going rule, the monks spent many a blissful day brewing ale, carousing in *The Frisky Friar Inn,* and trading in fake relics with the pilgrims who worshipped at the shrine of Saint Wilfred's bunion.

But life at the abbey was not always so comfortable. For Abbot Theodore was often far from home, spending much of his time up in London, hobnobbing at the Royal Court, and in his absence, Prior Solomon grasped the helm with a firmer hand. And then the monks would say their prayers and sing their psalms and starch the linen altar cloths until the abbot thundered home again on his trusty Arab steed.

Naturally there were those in the town of Saint Agnes Next-the-Sea who spoke against the monks and their worldly ways but they'd as well have saved their breath to cool their pottage. For the abbey owned the town, from every stinking hovel, wayside tavern and market stall, to the grandest merchants' houses that lined the bustling harbour where the River Twist poured into the ocean. And Brother Benedict, the greedy bursar, demanded rents and tithes from the poor without pity, sparing neither a skinny herring nor a heel of cheese for the lepers at the monastery gates.

Enough to stir up bad feeling, you might have thought, since so many depended on the abbey for their work – and then there was the small matter of little Obadiah Pug and the mishap with the bursar's lioness ... but that was a year ago and surely such tragedies are best forgotten.

It was a warm evening in late summer, just before the Lammas Day Fair. The hawthorn was bursting with rusty berries and fat blackbirds squatted in the spiky branches, gorging themselves in readiness for the harsh winter months. The vines were heavy with sweet grapes, the monks were brewing barley beer, and a symphony of blowflies buzzed drowsily over the dung heaps; but all was not as peaceful as it appeared at Saint Wilfred's Abbey. For Abbot Theodore had met with an accident.

Returning to Saint Agnes from London for the stag hunting, he had fallen from his Arab stallion as he was fording the River Twist. It was only the matter of a shattered kneecap – a trifling injury, you might have thought, for a hardened old soldier – but the Abbot was not in his first youth and the wound had begun to fester. No amount of bleeding and leeching seemed to cool his fever.

And, as if this were not trouble enough for the thirteenth-century abbey, young Brother Tom had taken a fancy to the miller's daughter, and old Brother Ethelwig was about to launch his flying-machine from the top of the bell tower.

Chapter 2

The Ornithopter

Brother Ethelwig, ancient keeper of the bells, perched on the parapet of the abbey tower, beating his wings impatiently. He strained against the rope that tethered him to the battlements, long muscular feet gripping the ramparts. The evening was warm and breezy; perfect conditions for flying.

"Hurry up, Pug," he bellowed to the belfry assistant over the booming of the wind. He pointed his eagle nose windward, two hundred dizzying feet above the sandstone walls of the abbey – above the monks in straw hats, crawling like black bees in the honey meadows and the tiny grey novices, playing leap-frog in the cloisters.

"Nearly there, sir," cried old Job, checking his master's leather harness and adjusting the scarlet tail feathers. "It's very windy!" he added anxiously, squinting west across the cloisters into the sun, already sinking in a rosy flush behind the watermill on the bow bend of the River Twist. "Maybe another day would be …"

"Nonsense, Pug," laughed the wiry old monk. "We have the best Chinese silk this time. I feel as light as a dandelion seed! Ready with the taper?"

"Ready when you are, sir," trembled Pug, struggling to keep the flame alight.

"Then hurry up!" he cried. "Ignite me! Wait for the up-draught – then launch the ornithopter!"

"Good luck, Brother Ethelwig. Remember what we said. Think up! Think elevate …"

"Think eagle!" cried Brother Ethelwig as he stretched his crimson wings and began a slow, rhythmic beating.

The wind sang in the bell ropes. Pug's hands shook only slightly as he held the glowing taper to the black powder in the crucible beneath the kite shaped tail. The wind dropped. For a solemn moment the trees stood still, quivering, like dancers waiting for the music to begin. And then on the up-draught, old Job Pug plunged his hand into the crucible. There was a hideous bang. Jackdaws exploded upwards in a cloud of wings, shrieking in terror as Brother Ethelwig shot over the abbey like a bolt from a crossbow, black smoke belching from the rear of his flying machine.

He whooped in triumph as he soared over the abbot's house, hawk's eyes picking out the infirmary below with its own neat herb garden, the beast house where the bursar kept his lion, strips of farm land the colour of saffron and burnt sugar, the dark scar of the forest and the turreted silhouette of the coastal town beyond. Gliding on the air currents, he swooped back towards the apple orchard along the leafy line of the River Twist that lay coiled like a silver serpent around the refectory wall.

But Job Pug, watching anxiously from the tower, saw that something was wrong. A small corner of scarlet silk seemed to be flapping free. He stared in horror as it gradually began to unpeel itself from the structure of twine and feathers. Brother Ethelwig twisted his neck sharply upwards, alarmed by a sudden sensation of losing height.

Everyone looked up, and afterwards everybody blamed Ethelwig; from the inky scribe for the ruby blot on his parchment, to the potter in the great court of the abbey, whose skewed jug would never grace the Lord of the Manor's table.

"Think eagle!" screamed Pug helplessly from the battlements as his beloved master was tossed upwards on a gust of wind, the loose wing silk streaking out like a blood red flag behind him. "Think up! Think elevate!" he wailed in bitter disappointment, as Brother Ethelwig spiralled wildly downwards, a brilliant tangle of ropes and pulleys, tumbling out of a pink and purple sky.

Tom Fletcher sat in the apple tree, his grey habit tucked up in his leather belt, sweet juice dribbling down his chin. The dusting of freckles on his nose had deepened in the summer sun, until now his face looked if someone had slipped with the nutmeg shaker. He leant his auburn head towards Bessie Miller, a shy look in his eyes, and then planted a quick kiss on her plump mouth.

"Tom!" she gasped, black eyes flashing. "You're a novice! I thought you weren't supposed to like girls. And anyway, you're all sticky," she grumbled, touching her mouth with the back of her hand.

Tom drew back, his face suddenly hot. "Who said anything about liking girls?" he mumbled, picking a scab on his knee. "And it's *Chief* novice, if you don't mind, Bessie," he corrected. "And also head chorister, to give me all my titles."

"You're only chief novice because you're the oldest," she said with a quick frown, as if the idea displeased her. "Not for any other reason."

Tom flung his apple core through the tangle of branches with a strangled groan. "Don't rub salt in my scabs! I'll be fourteen in a few months – old enough to take my vows – and then I really will be stuck in this place. I want to see the world, like Abbot Theodore ... Constantinople ... Jerusalem ... and just look at me – trapped here learning Latin with a bully of a novice master and his spiky cane."

He slapped his bottom with a grimace. Bessie giggled, looking up at him from under her long eyelashes. "It's not funny," scowled Tom. "You know Brother Dunstan's a real tyrant. He keeps his true nature in check when Abbot Theodore's around. But the abbot's very ill – haven't you heard? Heaven help us if Prior Solomon becomes abbot. The prior's not cruel but he's strict, and Brother Dunstan adores him." Tom hunched his shoulders and wrung his hands together, pursing his lips into a thin mean line in a perfect imitation of the novice master. *"Oh, Prior Solomon,"* he mimicked in a grovelling voice. *"Is there anything else you can think of to make the novices' lives more miserable? A smaller fire in their dormitory perhaps or a little extra ancient Greek?"*

Bessie clapped her hands in delight. Tom was a wonderful mimic. She could almost see the bland doughy face of the novice master, with its clammy sheen of perspiration, like a film of wax.

Tom gave Bessie a warning nudge as two pious novices in neat grey robes passed beneath the tree, their hands folded. They looked up suspiciously as the remains of the apple landed at their feet in a splatter of juice.

"Is that you, Brother Thomas?" called Brother Odo bossily, peering into the branches as the abbey bell chimed through the evening air. Tom bit on his knuckle, his hazel eyes stretched wide as he struggled to stifle a laugh. "He'll be late for Vespers again if he's not careful, won't he, Felix?" said Odo, in a voice meant for Tom.

Tom fingered his newly chipped tooth. It was still a bit wobbly, but at least he'd given Odo an eye like a damson in return for it. "Here's an idea," he whispered, brightening. "I'll buy a flock of sheep and take the wool to Flanders. Everyone wants English fleece these days. And when I've made my fortune, I'll come back and marry you, Bessie." His cheeks felt suddenly hot again. "I ... I mean," he added with a casual laugh, "nobody else would touch you with a pig stick!"

Bessie's dark curls quivered with indignation. "You can't suppose Father would let me marry you! He has no time for monks, along with everyone else in this town. Your fat bursar, Brother Benedict, has put up the rent for our mill again. And besides, *my* mother was Alice de Lacy before she became plain Mistress Miller. The de Lacys are noblemen," she preened, smoothing her tangled hair.

Tom wiped his sticky fingers on his robe, a sly look in his eye. "Come to think of it – why *did* your mother marry a humble miller?" he asked, regretting his spite as the barb hit home.

Bessie flinched. "Love, I suppose," she said uneasily, avoiding his eyes.

Tom raised one sarcastic eyebrow – he'd been practising the trick for weeks. *"Love?"* The word cracked in the middle and dropped a few tones. He winced. What on earth was wrong with his voice? Squeaky one minute and down in his boots the next. And he had a spot on his chin the size of a pea. He tried again. "Love? It would take more than love to make me leave a grand house like Micklow Manor for the Mill at Tirley Grange. Just think about it, Bessie. Sir Ranulf de Lacy is actually your grandfather and yet here you are, living in corn mill!"

Bessie gazed down at her homespun dress, a crease in her brow. "You know we never mention Sir Ranulf at home, Tom. I've never even spoken to him. Whenever I ask my parents about it they always clam up … change the subject …"

"Bessie – look!" shrieked Tom, nearly losing his balance on the branch. He scrambled up the gnarled trunk to get a better view of the plummeting scarlet object spinning out of control. "Oh Lord! It's Ethelwig again. We don't see him for days and then he comes tumbling out of the sky!"

Bessie covered her head, as a shower of twigs and acorns rained down. There was a sickening crunch and the sound of splintering wood as the wounded ornithopter burst through the branches of a nearby oak and came to a shuddering halt. Brother Ethelwig dangled limply below, upside down like a scarlet bat. His eagle nose had come to rest somewhere close to his left ear and his eyes were closed.

"Too many tail feathers," they heard him murmur as he twirled gently in the evening breeze. "That was my big mistake. And maybe I'd better think Buzzard next time."

Lammas Eve –
July 31st 1220

Chapter 3

The Rose of Damascus

Prior Solomon's smooth black hair was long, beneath the barest hint of a tonsure, his skin the colour of barley bread. He wore his beard in the eastern fashion, without a moustache. He could read the serpentine script of the Qur'an like a scholar, and ride an Arab stallion as well as any soldier. His Saracen mother had called him her beauty, her gift from Allah, but the townswomen of Saint Agnes Next-the-Sea thought his nose was too long to be called handsome – and besides, he held it too high.

Just how this exotic prior first came to the abbey of Saint Wilfred was a Crusader's tale. *"I might have left my eye behind at the siege of Acre,"* Abbot Theodore had laughed, as he quaffed French wine with Sir Ranulf de Lacy, the Lord of the Manor, *'but I've brought home a Muslim boy instead! Barely ten years old. Saw his parents massacred in front of the city walls. I took pity on the lad; he sailed back with me on The Lady Pilgrim."*

Sir Ranulf de Lacy slapped his thigh and reached for a dish of eels. *"So what will you do with him now, Theodore? I can't see you as a wet-nurse!"*

"Oh, I've already put him with the novice master," winked the abbot. *"I can't guarantee they'll make a Christian of him, but he'll learn how to brew ale – that's for sure!"*

The orphan boy did not forget the stories of his own religion, *The Tale of the Fish* and *The Queen and the Bird*, yet he listened owl-eyed to stories from the Bible, of loaves and fishes and water and wine, so that he no longer knew whether he was a Saracen or a Christian child. But all this was thirty summers ago, and as the seasons rolled round, the boy passed from grey novice to black robed monk, and from black monk to proud prior.

It was the day after Brother Ethelwig's fall from the sky, and Prior Solomon was vexed. Perhaps it was on account of the grave news of Abbot Theodore from Brother Silas, the monastery physician. The abbot's knee was no better – in truth it was worse, in spite of the application of a cockroach poultice. On the other hand, the prior was an ambitious man, and it was well known that he would be happy to slip his feet into the abbot's empty sandals when the time was right. So maybe something else was bothering him. Perhaps it was the letter that he clutched indignantly in his hand, so that if his long elegant fingers had not been so brown, his knuckles would have been white.

Prior Solomon strode furiously towards the door of his comfortable study and twisted the key in the lock. His thin black brows formed an arrow of annoyance as his eyes scanned the writing one last time. Then, with trembling fingers, he held the thick yellow parchment towards the candle flame. The edge of the letter glowed orange and white smoke curled over his hand as the parchment burned swiftly to a white ash that settled gently on his black habit, like flakes of grubby snow. At the last possible moment, he dropped the remaining fragment onto the rush floor and stamped hard, grinding it beneath his silken slipper.

He jumped like a startled deer. A rumpus outside the window. He opened the horn shutters just a chink and peered out. It was hot – another stifling day, and there was the fool Ethelwig again, and that irksome novice with him.

The prior's nose lengthened as he watched Brother Thomas scrambling up the mangled oak, where the ornithopter had crash-landed the evening before. *Why wasn't the ruffian at Latin? The boy was growing wilder by the day, without the help of that buffoon Ethelwig.*

"I'm doing my best, Ethelwig," shouted Tom from the top of the tree. "It's awfully tangled."

Prior Solomon sucked in his breath. Bessie Miller was ducking hurriedly through the orchard towards the tree. *That girl seems to come and go as she pleases,* he thought disapprovingly, *with her skirt rucked up and her brown legs bare. To be sure, her father grinds the abbey corn, but the wench is a young woman now – not a lisping toddler any longer, nursing a straw doll.*

Tom shinned down the mossy trunk to greet Bessie, his cheeks the colour of the cherry silk he held bunched in his arms. The prior sniffed. *Flying-machines! Moon-eyed novices! Abbot Theodore has a lot to answer for.* "I must speak to the novice master about young Thomas," he muttered grimly. "It's time that chief novice of ours took his vows – and a warning word in the miller's ear about his daughter wouldn't go amiss either."

"There are white sails on the horizon!" Bessie shouted breathlessly, her hand to her chest. "Father says it looks like *The Rose of Damascus*."

"*The Rose of Damascus!*" cried Tom, dropping the silk at Ethelwig's feet. "I'll run and fetch Brother Benedict from the beast house straight away. If it really is *The Rose of Damascus* – the bursar's expecting a Caladrius!"

Chapter 4

The Caladrius

Brother Benedict's bulbous eyes squinted through a cat's cradle of masts and rigging towards the slowly approaching ship, crammed with silks and exotic spices from the bazaars of Alexandria and Baghdad. He clutched a volume of *Pliny's Natural History* tight in his hand. As the vessel loomed larger, Tom joined an excited crowd of merchants on the jetty amongst the dull bales of English wool awaiting the outgoing tide. He was thrilled to be missing Latin. *"Brother Benedict's orders,"* he'd smirked cheekily, as he fled from the purple fury of the novice master and his twitching birch twig cane.

"What's taking so long?" roared the thick-necked bursar, heaving sweatily up the ship's gangplank as soon as it was lowered onto dry land. "I'm paying a king's ransom for this creature, I'll have you know!" he grumbled, his undershot jaw jutting.

"No land lubbers on board," snapped the Captain, barring his way. "Silks and spices off first. Livestock's in the bowels of the ship!"

He shoved Brother Benedict hard, sending the barrel-chested monk reeling into a pile of lobster pots. The children cheered, but the townspeople shifted uneasily. The bursar had been as unpopular as the plague in the town for many a long year, but since the incident with the boy and the lioness, dislike had rubbed shoulders with dread.

"Wait 'til you see what the devil's ordered this time!" muttered a toothless mate in wide sailor's trousers, ducking as a roll of Turkey carpet passed over his head. Expectant whispers rustled amongst the spectators on the quayside.

"Last time it was an elephant. And before that, a bear!"

"Shouldn't be allowed, I say. Who does he think he is? The King himself!"

Some said Brother Benedict had ordered a leopard, to rival King Henry's in London. It was rumoured he even kept a tiger, but no one had seen it arrive.

Tom was struggling to help the bursar to his feet, when he heard a horrified gasp, rippling through the mass of bodies crammed along the water's edge. Brother Benedict's hard little eyes swivelled in the direction of the hubbub. A Venetian merchant stood on the jetty beside a wooden cage. It was heaving to and fro as the furious cargo flapped its wild white wings, squawking in a frenzy of rage and terror and kicking at the bars with sturdy red legs. The crowd parted as Brother Benedict thundered through, his mottled neck as broad as the crown of his head, thick red lips parted expectantly. He stopped suddenly, frowning in suspicion at the waddling creature, stalking up and down the cage on knobbly purple feet.

"Where's my Caladrius?" he bellowed, staring past the jolting cage and gazing anxiously up and down the harbour.

"You may take the fiend and welcome," spat the merchant in thickly accented tones, shrinking away from the animal smell that clung to the bursar's robes. "You lucky I didn't toss evil creature into sea – the racket she is making on this voyage!"

Brother Benedict's eyes popped. "You double-crossing dervish!" he cried, leafing violently through the illustrations in his book. "I ordered a Caladrius!"

"And that is exactly what I am delivering," replied the arrogant Venetian over his shoulder as he turned away from the hissing bird with its quivering black tongue.

"But … but … it's hideous," blustered Brother Benedict. "A Caladrius should be beautiful!" He brandished the picture in the air so the crowd could see. "Graceful neck … slender legs … elegant beak …"

"That is a picture painted by … by … *ignoramus*!" scoffed the merchant with a dismissive wave of his hand. "And anyway," he cried, beginning to enjoy the attention of the rabble on the quayside, "who knows? Maybe this Caladrius feels the same way about you! Perhaps you are not the only one who is a little … how do you say it? Disappointed?"

The houses of the rich merchants hugged the docks, only slightly grander than the prosperous stone dwellings of the Jewish moneylenders behind. Tom was finding it hard to negotiate the narrow alleys of the town with the lurching cage balanced on a small wheelbarrow, but any interest in the Caladrius in the Jewish Quarter was confined to a gleam of a candle through a chink in a firmly closed shutter. There was an eerie silence in Jewry Lane. Tom shivered in spite of the heat. The Jews had kept more than ever to themselves since the riots of the previous winter. Even so, he felt their watchful eyes upon him, though nobody crept out for a look.

But the rest of Saint Agnes was a different story. Word had spread like a forest fire, and as tile and stone gave way to thatch and timber, curious heads emerged from windows, shutters flung back. So by the time Tom trundled his barrow past the tall cross in the market square he had recovered his flagging spirits. It was hotter than ever, but as he tucked up his cassock and rolled back his sleeves, he noticed the sky was darkening. He slid an uneasy glance at the bursar, stomping along beside the barrow with a face like the thunder they could sense in the air.

"I still say it's repulsive," raged Brother Benedict, "and I'm not paying a penny for it."

"Mmm – it is disgusting," said Tom, peering admiringly into the cage. "Is it true what they say? Can it really predict life and death? You could try it out on Abbot Theodore …"

Brother Benedict wrinkled his wide nostrils. "Hmm," he replied doubtfully. "I suppose if it does what it's supposed to do …"

"I'm sure if you don't want it, Brother Silas will take it for the infirmary," said Tom mischievously. "You know … if it can really absorb the fever of a dying man ..."

"Who said I didn't want it?" snapped Benedict, shooting a possessive glance through the wooden slats of the crate. "Silas can keep his grasping hands off my Caladrius. Our physician is doing well enough for himself selling his pills and powders in the town, although he should be more careful with his poisonous potions if you ask me. Abbot Theodore seems to be getting worse in his care, not better," he added darkly. "Yes. Things will change at Saint Wilfred's when I'm abbot. I'll put a stop to Silas and his swindling ways, not to mention Ethelwig and his flying machines," he snarled, slapping the cage hard with the flat of his hand. The Caladrius squawked in terror. Brother Benedict smiled; his expression almost fond. "Its feet are a pretty colour – I'll say that for it."

They were approaching the outskirts of the town, where wattle and daub hovels straggled along the edge of a rough track, smoke spiralling from holes in the roofs into the inky sky.

"You can help me shut the animals up in the beast house when we get back to the abbey," grunted the bursar, as a jagged fork of lightning split the clouds. "There's nothing Delilah hates more than thunder."

"But I have to go to choir practise now," said Tom. "Brother Fergus is entering the trebles for the ballad competition at the Lammas Fair."

The bursar made a choking sound in his throat. "Well Brother Fergus and his 'trilling trebles' will have to wait. Delilah gnawed right through the bars last time we had a storm!"

The beast house lay on the southern bank of the River Twist, a muddled assortment of enclosures and pens, much too close to the dormitories for the comfort of the monks, who complained of the stench in the day and the roaring at night.

Delilah was feeling uneasy. She padded restlessly up and down her cage, her breathing strangely rapid – her heartbeat a little too fast. The incessant grumbling from around the valley was making her nervous. She felt that curious pricking beneath her skin that she always sensed when the sky turned dark in the daytime – and besides, her belly was empty. She paused, one huge paw raised, head on one side, ears pricked. Her velvet nostrils flared in recognition. There it was again – that delicious odour that brought the juices flooding to her mouth. *What could possibly smell so sweet?* She licked her smooth black lips with a rough red tongue as the source of the smell staggered into view, wheeling a barrow with a birdcage on top.

"Where do you want the crate, Brother Benedict?" puffed Tom, wiping his brow.

"I'll take the Caladrius now," wheezed the bursar, grasping the handles of the barrow. "You give Delilah her dinner. She's in her sleeping area. I'll close the gate – keep her trapped inside whilst you rush in and put the offal down."

"M ... me?" stammered Tom in horror.

"Well I can't see anybody else around," retorted Brother Benedict sarcastically, pretending to look behind him.

"B ... but I thought the abbot said ... I mean I thought we weren't allowed ... you know ... after what happened to little Obadiah Pug ..." he gulped, taking a step backwards as the bursar's face passed from its usual puce to a thunderous crimson. Delilah growled hungrily.

"What happened to that Pug boy was his own brainless blunder," snapped Brother Benedict, as the first fat drop of rain plopped between his eyes. "He should have moved faster! That witless child got no more than he deserved, as I told Prior Solomon when old Job Pug complained. Now shift yourself or it will be Obadiah Pug for breakfast and Brother Thomas for supper. She'd find you sweeter than hogs' livers I'll be bound ... now that she's got a taste for boy flesh!"

Chapter 5

The Poisonous Beast

Tom fled thankfully through the warm rain, across the bridge and into the infirmary passage that led to the abbey church, the stink of the offal bucket still in his nostrils and the bursar's taunts in his ears. He leant, trembling, against the cool wall, his stomach heaving. *"A taste for boy flesh!"* He was badly shaken.

The voices of his friends fluted comfortingly from the abbey. He should really go straight to choir practice. He didn't want to let Brother Fergus down, but it would take more than ballads to lighten his mood after the beast house. Pushing himself reluctantly from the wall, he began to drag his feet in the direction of the singing. *I am Head Chorister, I suppose,* he thought grudgingly, *but then again I also have duties as Chief Novice. It's surely my job to tell the physician about the Caladrius right away.* Tom paused at a bend in the passage. He couldn't get the Caladrius out of his head. He fingered his pimple with a thoughtful frown. *After all, I do have a responsibility towards Abbot Theodore,* he convinced himself, as he spun slowly on his heel. *I might even be able to help him."* "And besides," he muttered decisively, "there really is something wrong with my voice!" With a determined sniff, he began to walk briskly in the opposite direction.

Yellow smoke billowed from a flask on an iron tripod as Tom poked his nose around the pharmacy door. He stared in alarm as the globular mixture began to fizz up in the jar. It juddered violently for a moment, then all of a sudden there was an ear-splitting BANG! Shards of glass like tiny arrows splintered across the room in a cloud of orange steam. Tom dived under a table, covering his head. Hard objects clunked down from above. Something wet and slimy splattered on his cheek and began to slide slowly down his neck. He froze in disgust as a dead toad slithered down his body and plopped gently onto the floor. He waited until the sound of tumbling objects had stopped and then crawled cautiously from his hiding place.

A heap of smoking rags lay humped in the middle of the floor, amongst the smouldering rushes and the shattered remains of a jar of pickled vipers. As Tom looked on in alarm, the bundle of cloth rose up, transforming itself as if by magic into Brother Silas, the monastery physician. Tom took a step backwards, engulfed by a smell of rotten eggs.

"Oh no! Poor Osbert!" exclaimed the physician, his eyes on the mangled toad. "He was a wonderful source of amphibian spittle." He started, as if noticing Tom for the first time. "Now what do you want?" he snapped.

"*The Rose of Damascus* has docked," blurted Tom, "and Brother Benedict's bought a Caladrius!"

"A Caladrius?" breathed Brother Silas, his yellow eyes gleaming with sudden interest. "Are you quite sure? But what perfect timing. I have only set eyes on a Caladrius once in my life – at the medical school in Salerno as a young man."

"I thought it might help Abbot Theodore ... it's very ugly ..."

"Oh they are," nodded the physician with enthusiasm. "Exquisitely hideous. But you may be right – this could be the answer to our prayers. Abbot Theodore is not responding to my remedies ..."

"So it's true? The abbot really is dying?"

"Maybe the Caladrius can help where my treacle has failed," murmured Brother Silas, hurriedly fitting a circular piece of rabbit skin over his wrinkled tonsure. "The bird is reputed to have power to turn sickness into health, but only if it will gaze upon the sufferer. If it will not, then the patient will surely die. I have been longing to see such a thing again for more than forty years. Now, pass me my cloak," he said, clicking his fingers at a mound of moth-eaten fabric draped over a desk.

As Tom picked up the filthy garment, he couldn't help noticing an astrological chart, scrawled all over with signs of the zodiac. Brother Silas had inscribed Prior Solomon's name at the top under the title 'Horoscope' but it was the margins that attracted Tom's attention. They were covered in a mass of doodles in a variety of handwriting –

Abbot Silas   **Abbot Silas**   *Abbot Silas*

"I'll take that, thank you!" rapped Silas, snatching the parchment from under Tom's nose and twisting it into a tight roll. He wound his tattered cloak around his body like a bandage around a mummy. "Now, where did I put the abbot's medicine?" He stalked around Tom on skinny heron's legs. "*Theriac*, the ancients called it," he said peering at the thick brown treacle that clung lumpily to the sides of the flask. "Otherwise known as the *poisonous beast*. Cures everything from corns to constipation!"

Tom raised an eyebrow. "But if it cures everything," he ventured, "why would you need a Caladrius?"

Brother Silas shot Tom a furious glance. "Enough of your cheek, young man," he snapped tartly. "You have a most peculiar talent for turning up where you're least wanted. Now be off with you! I'm away to the beast house. I must examine this rare specimen right away."

The Caladrius opened a malicious eye and glared at Brother Benedict in the light of a stinking tallow candle. It was raining hard now, and the beast house roof was leaking. The creature shuffled awkwardly along its perch, flexing its knobbly feet. It was as ugly a fowl as you could wish to see, except for its feathers, which were as white as an altar cloth.

"Come Jezebel, come my beauty," crooned the bursar. He extended his arm encased in a hunting gauntlet, criss-crossed with deep gashes where the bird's hooked bill had already lacerated the leather. "It seems we need your help already," he murmured fondly as the bird waddled clumsily onto the leather glove, "and to think that you have only just come to us."

The bursar turned sharply at the sound of a footfall. Brother Silas was approaching the beast house door, a storm lantern held aloft, his eager face shining wet in its glow.

"News spreads fast, Brother Physician," said the bursar coldly, stroking the bird's snowy back.

The lamplight flared on Brother Silas's hollow cheeks and deep set eyes, betraying the skull beneath the skin. Without a word of greeting, he rushed greedily towards the Caladrius, his covetous eyes caressing each feather from cruel beak to horny toes.

"Give it to me!" demanded Silas, thrusting out a skinny arm. "It could not have arrived at a more auspicious time. Abbot Theodore is weakening by the hour. This creature is perfect – exactly what I need."

Brother Benedict drew back possessively, half turning so that his body was between the physician and the Caladrius.

"But how can this be, Brother Silas?" he asked slyly over his shoulder. "You told me yourself after Prime this morning that you have been treating the abbot with your own special cure."

"I have done everything in my power to help our dear abbot," replied the physician with thinly veiled dislike, "but the knee is rotting and the poison creeps from limb to limb. Prior Solomon is with him now, keeping vigil until I return, but I fear the patient is rapidly slipping beyond human help."

Brother Benedict raised a sceptical eyebrow. "I must confess it seems a little odd to me that the abbot's knee began to fester *after* the administration of your treacle."

"Meaning what, precisely?" snapped the physician, eyes like stones.

"Meaning nothing at all," replied the bursar holding his gaze with an icy smile, "except that I know you to be an ambitious man."

Brother Silas froze, his fists clenched – knuckles like bone. "You may imply what you please." His voice was white with rage. "But you can prove nothing. And as for ambition, you are not without aspirations yourself I believe, *Brother* Bursar."

"My job, my dear Silas, is to keep the finances of this abbey in good order," replied the bursar. "For myself, I have every hope that Prior Solomon will be elected abbot of Saint Wilfred's in the event of ..." He paused. "But let us not be too hasty. Abbot Theodore might yet recover ... unless, of course, you have reason to know otherwise."

"You should guard your evil tongue," snarled Silas, his voice trembling as the rain thrummed on the beast house roof. "Do you suppose I do not understand your spiteful insinuations?" Brother Silas lowered his voice. "But you have gone too far this time, Benedict," he rasped savagely. "Your allegation is serious – and not one that I am minded to forgive."

Abbot Theodore's room is dim. A bowl of honey stands on the broad window sill – a sweet alluring death-trap, black with the bodies of unwary summer wasps. The sky outside is heavy with rain. Within the sickroom the air is thick, drenched with the fetid stench of fast approaching death. Prior Solomon kneels by the dying abbot's bed, his noble forehead bowed in prayer. Four candles burn at four corners of the straw pallet on which the abbot lies.

Prior Solomon leans forward, his ear to the old man's mouth. The abbot is trying to speak. "Hush, my Lord Abbot," he murmurs gently. "Conserve your strength for the trial to come ..."

But Abbot Theodore shakes his head, fighting for breath through lips that are cracked and dry. "It is too late for trials, my son," he gasps. "My light is fading fast. But attend to me while I have breath to speak. It is my dying wish that you should succeed me as abbot of Saint Wilfred's, for you are my son in all but blood. I was not a fit man to be abbot of this abbey – but you can gather the wayward flock that I have allowed to stray. When I rescued you as a boy from the burning city of Acre and brought you here – I intended you for this."

Prior Solomon looks up gravely. Is there a glint of a tear in his eye for the brave crusader who saved a motherless child from certain death those long years ago, or is it the smoke from the oil lamp that stings his eyes? The abbot's voice is fainter now so that Prior Solomon has to rest his head on the pillow to hear the whispered words.

"I am a sinner, a warrior at heart and a man of the world. But you will make a fine successor to me. We are as different as the sun and the moon, as fire and water. But who knows," he rasps, a ghost of a smile in his feeble voice, "perhaps the new abbot may find it in his heart to say a prayer ... for a wicked old soldier who once loved an orphan boy as if he were his son."

Chapter 6

The Angel of Death

Brother Fergus's habit was far too short. He wore it that way for convenience, for Fergus was a Scot and dancing was his passion. *"There's no finer pair of legs in Saint Wilfred's,"* he would boast, and indeed it was difficult to imagine a better pair of calves: muscular, peppered with freckles and hairy as caterpillars.

As Brother Benedict was following the physician to the abbot's house with the Caladrius, Brother Fergus's legendary legs were busily engaged in dancing a reel. A group of six novices of assorted sizes were doing the same, their habits hitched into their leather belts. In and out of the choir stalls they whirled, arms linked, legs flying, with Fergus's shaggy lurcher, Mungo, snapping at their heels. The wind in the belfry could scarcely be heard above the scraping of a bony young novice on a fiddle and the plaintive wheezing of the hurdy gurdy organ as Brother Edmund, the smallest of them all, ground on its handle as if his own breath depended on it.

"Och, Brother Herbert, that was my in-growing toenail ye just stepped on!" cried Brother Fergus good-naturedly, swinging his clumsy partner, his russet hair fizzing around the edges of his tonsure. He glanced expectantly towards the door. "Where's our friend Tom, by the way? I'll have a crow to pluck with him if he's not here on time for rehearsal." He laughed indulgently. "That rascal tries even the patience of a saint like me. Careful over there!" he cried as a pair of novices tumbled to the floor in a tangle of sandals. "Not so vigorous now, boys!"

"Our robes are too long," puffed one of them, scrambling to his feet and stuffing his habit into his woollen under breeches.

"I am sacrist of this abbey, young man," puffed Brother Fergus, wiping the perspiration from his brow with the corner of the altar cloth, "not novice master. I am in charge of gold plate, chalices and the precious relic of Saint Wilfred's bunion – not garments for wee ones!"

"And when did you last see a chalice, eh Fergus?" laughed Ethelwig, hobbling into the nave of the church and warding off Mungo's slobbering tongue with his stick. He was carrying a mysterious contraption under his arm. "You seem to keep those treasures hidden away from one Lammastide to the next."

Brother Fergus smiled mischievously. "Aye Ethelwig, there's a lot tae be said for an abbot who does nae care for Matins and Vespers and allows us to talk in the refectory."

Ethelwig fingered his swollen nose. "It's no joking matter, Fergus. Lord help us if Abbot Theodore dies and Prior Solomon becomes abbot. There'll be a change of regime, I can promise you that – and it will be more drudgery than dancing I can assure you."

"Och now Ethelwig, dunnae be dismal now. We'll mount that midden heap when we come to it. For my part I've a deal more faith in old Silas and his crushed snails than you have. Now what have ye brought me today, my friend?"

"The Octomanipulator!" announced Ethelwig proudly. "There are eight wooden hands for eight books of music. At the simple twist of one handle – all the pages turn over at once."

Fergus slapped Ethelwig on the back. "You are a genius, Ethelwig! It's just the boost we need. We're entering the choir for the ballad contest at the fair tomorrow, and we cannae have the wee nuns frae Saint Hilda's beating us again this year. Come and have a look at this lads," he called to the novices, who had just started a game of football with a hog's bladder.

As the eager novices crowded round Ethelwig, Tom popped his head cautiously around the chapel door, squinting into the shadowy candlelight. "Psst! Herbert! Over here."

Herbert spun round to see Tom beckoning frantically, his finger to his lips. He glanced quickly over his shoulder, but the novices were busy fighting over Ethelwig's new invention.

"Steady on, boys!" cried Ethelwig. "You'll tear it to pieces before you've tried it out."

Herbert hurried breathlessly to the door, his round face glowing with perspiration. "Where've you been?" he whispered. "Brother Fergus has been asking for you."

"Quick," said Tom, pulling Herbert's robe. "I've got something to show you. I'll explain as we go."

But the Caladrius was not on its perch when they reached the beast house. Its heavy silver chain swung gently in the draught that blew through the ramshackle planks of the walls. Tom groaned. "They must have left for the abbot's house already. Brother Silas couldn't wait to try it out. Come on. Follow me."

"But we can't go after them to the abbot's house ..." protested Herbert, hanging back.

"Of course we can. I came to fetch you specially, didn't I?" said Tom in exasperation. "Don't you want to see it? I'll go on my own if you don't come now. I'm not missing this for all the wool in Flanders!"

The door to the abbot's house was ajar. Tom slipped through, grabbed a pewter candlestick and made straight for the stone stairs, which wound steeply upwards to the floor above. Herbert lagged behind, wiping the rain from his face. He stared in wonder at the embroidered wall hangings, cushioned chairs and silver dishes full of summer fruits. "How do you know the way?" he whispered.

Tom's foot was already on the bottom step. "Because I've been in here before, of course." He rolled his eyes in frustration. "Don't look so shocked – only a little visit when the abbot was away. Now, come *on!*"

The boys climbed in silence to the top of the stairs,

Tom's skinny shadow preceding Herbert's bulkier one on the ceiling above. They paused. A murmur of low voices floated from beyond the open door of the abbot's chamber. Tom handed the candlestick to Herbert shakily, surprised at the thumping of his own heart. Herbert held his breath as he watched Tom creep towards the flickering arc of candlelight that spilled onto the landing, then gathering his courage, he tip-toed after Tom across the rush strewn floor.

Tom peered warily around the door, a knot in his stomach. Prior Solomon was kneeling beside Abbot Theodore, crisp black head bowed beneath a fine tapestry of a stag hunt, in the place where a crucifix should have been. Brother Silas stood at the foot of the bed, the Caladrius perched on his arm – Brother Benedict a little apart, toad's eyes swivelling warily from the Caladrius to the kneeling figure of the prior, and then back to Brother Silas again.

Brother Silas looks just like a vulture, thought Tom. He swallowed hard. He could feel Herbert's breath on the back of his neck. "Can you see it?" he breathed, shrinking back to give Herbert a peep. "Don't let them see you."

"It is time, Prior Solomon," came the physician's voice through the doorway, his fingers fumbling with the linen cowl that covered the bird's snowy head. "I have done everything in my power to save Abbot Theodore's life …"

Herbert stifled a groan as Tom squashed his toe. "Move, you great lump!" hissed Tom. "I can't see through you." They watched in silence as Prior Solomon rose wearily to his feet, forming an elegant sign of the cross above the bed. "Then God's will be done," said the prior, as Brother Silas solemnly slipped off the hood.

The repulsive creature opened and closed its yellow beak several times. It blinked in the candlelight, tongue quivering like a thick black leech, a strange hissing sound issuing from its open bill.

Tom could feel Herbert's nails, digging into his flesh through his thin robe, as the Caladrius slowly began to turn its head – away from the dying abbot, away from the brooding Brothers in the putrid room. Slowly, slowly it swivelled its ugly beak towards Tom and Herbert as they crouched in the shadow of the half open door. Then arching its wild white wings like the Angel of Death, the hideous bird let forth a scream – a chilling sound that would have stopped the heart of the Devil himself.

Brother Silas was motionless, eyes fixed on the abbot's pallet, his face like bleached bone. Prior Solomon fell to his knees by the still body, a strangled sob in his throat. But Brother Benedict's eyes were shining, not with tears but with triumph.

The horrifying shriek of the Caladrius rang in the boys' ears as they raced from the abbot's house, leaping and squelching over the deep puddles left in the wake of the storm, splattering their habits with thick black mud. The soprano voices of the choristers echoed around the cloisters as the boys skidded in their sodden sandals towards the brightly lit windows of the chapel. Slithering to a halt by the arched opening that led to the choir, they leant panting against a stone buttress. "That was really horrible!" puffed

Herbert, pressing a stitch in his side.

Tom nodded, gasping for breath, but his eyes glittered in the moonlight. He was oddly thrilled in spite of everything, but there was something else too – a strange sense of foreboding that was growing stronger by the minute. "That hideous screech," he panted. "I've never heard anything so terrifying in my life. And did you notice, Herbert?" he added, swallowing a shudder. "When the Caladrius turned its ugly head – it looked directly at us!"

Tom and Herbert slipped through the sacristy passage and into the choir stalls. The novices had just reached the last verse of *'Katie Brewer with the Silver Eye',* and Brother Fergus's eyes were full of tears as the boys' shrill voices rose to a crescendo. Tom nudged the nearest novice, and whispered in his ear. The boy stopped singing and muttered to his neighbour, who leant towards the grubby neck of the next chorister. The news rippled down the row, as one by one the voices of the novices died away, until only young Edmund was still singing ... and then he too faltered, blushing, to a halt. It took Brother Fergus a full half minute to register that something was wrong. He opened his eyes, arms poised in mid-air, an astonished frown on his face.

"What in the name of heaven is the matter?" he asked in an offended tone. "This is the climax of the whole ballad!" He suddenly noticed Tom, hovering at the side of the choir stalls. "Ah, Brother Thomas," he said sarcastically. "You've joined us at last! We must thank our head chorister, boys, for sparing a wee moment of his precious time to attend choir practice." He paused, waiting for the usual sniggers, but nobody laughed. Brother Fergus raised a puzzled eyebrow. "Why? What is amiss? Young Edmund over there. Perhaps *you* can enlighten me."

Brother Edmund flushed to the tips of his ears. He had to stand on his tip-toes to see over the edge of the choir stalls, even with the aid of a nearby bolster. "I ... I'm sorry, Brother Fergus," stammered the little novice, his blond curls quivering with alarm. "We've just heard some dreadful news. It's Abbot Theodore. He's dead!"

Chapter 7

The Frisky Friar

Golden lantern light spilled down the wide stone steps of *The Frisky Friar Inn,* beneath the twisted vines above the door, as Brother Ethelwig hobbled into the low beamed parlour, leaning heavily on the arm of his belfry assistant, Job Pug. The news of Abbot Theodore's death had broken, and up at the monastery Prior Solomon was in sober conference with the senior monks. But down in the town, the tavern was a riot of life and colour – merchants and pilgrims, hawkers and traders, all gathered for the Lammas Fair the next day.

The broad-bottomed landlord squeezed between elegant stomachs clad in oriental damask and the bellies of stocky farm workers in homespun linen. He was carrying leather tankards of barley beer to a group of novices who were gathered around Brother Fergus and his dog at a low table, discussing the latest news.

"Oh *please* let us sing at the Lammas fair tomorrow,

Brother Fergus," pleaded the youngest novice. "I'm word perfect on my solo and you promised we'd beat *The Singing Sisters* from Saint Hilda's this year."

"I'm sorry, young Edmund," said Brother Fergus, patting his curly head fondly. "You can rest assured that I'm as disappointed as you are. You sing like an angel and *The Saint Wilfred Warblers* have never stood a better chance of seizing the prize, but it wouldnae be seemly to perform at the fair the very day after the death of our dear abbot."

Tom was lounging against a wall sucking gloomily on a plum stone. He couldn't get the shriek of the Caladrius out of his ears and now it seemed they'd be missing the Lammas Fair. Even the sight of Bessie Miller slicing up an oyster pie wasn't having its usual charm.

"I expect Brother Silas will go the fair, whatever's happened at the abbey," said Tom despondently. "I can't see him missing out on a chance to sell his cures. And Brother Benedict's planning elephant rides. What's the betting he'll be there too? It will be just us novices stuck at Saint Wilfred's – doing extra Greek with Brother Dunstan I shouldn't wonder … and thinking about death."

Mungo's tail thumped hard on the rushes as Brother Ethelwig and Job Pug made their way to the table.

"No Mistress Pug this evening, Job?" said Tom, dragging his eyes from Bessie's corner of the room.

There was a strained silence. Ethelwig glanced reproachfully at Tom as old Job began to settle his master into a low chair, fussily plumping up the feather cushions around him.

"Not tonight," replied Job curtly, drawing up a stool for

himself. "She's gone to visit her mother. Tomorrow will be a year to the day since little Obadiah … you know … and Mistress Pug … well … she's not feeling too jaunty." His fingers drifted wistfully to a small bone whistle around his neck – the last gift from Obadiah to his old father.

"I'm surprised to see you in *The Frisky Friar* this evening, Fergus," said Ethelwig, with a tactful change of subject. "Shouldn't you be in urgent conference with Prior Solomon? There'll have to be an election for a new abbot, you know lads," he said, nodding at the novices. "The Bishop will come down from London."

"Now why should they want me there, Ethelwig?" said Brother Fergus, shaking his head. "I'm hardly in the running for abbot of Saint Wilfred's."

"I think they should choose Brother Ethelwig," laughed Bessie, whirling past with a tray of oysters. "*Abbot* Ethelwig," she giggled, tossing her curls.

"Or you, Brother Fergus," said one of his choristers loyally. "Brother Fergus would get our vote, wouldn't he Tom?"

The boys glanced at their chief novice for approval. Everyone knew Tom adored Brother Fergus. They seemed to be modelled from the same clay, and it was not just the ginger hair and freckles. It was more of a wild exuberance – a rowdy delight in living.

But Tom was oblivious to their chatter. Bessie's mother had just squeezed into the parlour on her husband's arm, strands of golden hair escaping from under her wimple. She seemed much too young to be married to old Gabriel Miller and have to go about with her hair covered.

"Prior Solomon will surely be the new abbot," said Herbert. "He's always taken charge when Abbot Theodore's been away … and he does have some supporters …"

"Like who? Brother Dunstan?" scoffed Tom, turning back to his friends at the table. "He'll be more bullying than ever if Prior Solomon becomes abbot. Have you noticed? Our novice master's even grown his beard long to copy Prior Solomon and he's shaved off his moustache too!"

"Aye well," said Brother Fergus in mock regret. "It will take a deal more than that to improve the resemblance. You can arrange your facial hair all you like but there's little tae be done with a nose like a dumpling that's been in the pot too long!"

The novices collapsed in giggles.

"You'll have to polish up the altarpieces, Fergus, if Solomon's elected abbot," warned Ethelwig. "Get out all the golden goblets – and you boys will have to swap ballads for plainsong!"

"What about Brother Silas for abbot?" said Herbert. "That would be scary. Tom caught him practising his signature – *Abbot Silas* written in twenty different styles!"

Ethelwig sniffed. "And how in heaven's name would that black magician find time? He's too busy bottling up potions to sell at every Saint's Day fair in the neighbourhood. And anyway – I thought he'd sold his soul to the devil! Hardly a suitable choice …"

"Brother Benedict wants the job too," said Tom. He pressed his nostrils into a pig's snout. *"Things will change when I'm abbot,"* he mimicked, speaking through his nose.

"You should join a troop of mummers, young Tom – shouldn't he Fergus?" said Ethelwig with a chuckle.

But Brother Fergus's face had flushed with sudden anger. "Well I'm glad ye all find the bursar so amusing," he snarled, "but ye can rest assured that I do not!"

There was an uneasy silence. Ethelwig raised a hairy eyebrow. The parlour was growing hotter, candle smoke hovering in blue layers between the rush floor and the low raftered ceiling.

"Did I hear my friend the bursar mentioned?" came a hearty voice from behind the monks. Tom twisted round to see Gabriel Miller at his shoulder. "I've heard the sad news about Abbot Theodore, Brothers. I'm come to say I'm sorry. I've no love for the abbey as everyone knows, but Abbot Theodore was a brave soldier ..."

"We were discussing who the new abbot might be," said Tom.

"Aye and there's some of our company that think it's a joking matter," snapped Brother Fergus, glowering in Tom's direction.

Tom lowered his eyes with a frown. It wasn't like Fergus to be so tetchy. *I didn't mean any harm,* he thought, irritably. *I was only saying what everyone knows already.* All the same, he wished he'd kept his mouth shut.

Brother Fergus scraped back his stool and rose angrily to his feet, his short habit swinging at mid-calf. "Come, Mungo," he said with a slap on the dog's rump. "If ye'll excuse me friends, I'll be wending my way."

"What did I say?" shrugged Tom, staring after Brother Fergus as he thrust through the mass of bodies.

"You touched a tender spot, young man, that's all," said the miller. "God knows I have no love for the greedy bursar any more than old Job Pug here – but Brother Fergus has his own reasons for hating him."

The air was cool outside *The Frisky Friar*. Brother Fergus stood on the steps, bile rising in his throat, a breathless feeling in his chest. Something cold and wet pushed into his hand. He jerked impatiently away from Mungo's nose, as waves of painful memories washed over him; scenes from that freezing winter night only eight months ago, when the people of Saint Agnes had set upon the moneylenders – the night when all Jewry burned. He closed his eyes and gave in to the memories.

"The vermin are here!" Brother Benedict had cried in triumph, his eyes alight with vengeful glee, as he flung wide the sacristy door, a flaming brand in his hand.

"For God's sake, Benedict, have pity!" screamed Brother Fergus, battling with the door. "There are women and children. What harm have they ever done you?"

They huddled behind the sacrist, shivering in the winter vestry; the Rabbi, the goldsmith, the pawnbroker, crouched between piles of altar cloths and images of unknown saints, white breath pale as smoke. The children squeezed their eyes tight shut, mouthing a silent prayer to their God.

Brother Fergus could hear the baying mob of townspeople, already hammering at the abbey gates, brimming with ale and indignation. He had seen them from the bell tower, swarming up the well-worn track from the town, faces livid in the flickering torchlight, pitchforks waving. He had seen the rosy light in the sky above the town, as the pyres blazed in the market square, self-righteous flames devouring the scrolls of heathen scriptures and the evidence of a hundred unredeemed debts.

"I promised them sanctuary!" pleaded Brother Fergus. "This is a House of God! Ye'll have murder on your conscience, Benedict. I beg you, dunnae turn them out!"

Shouldering Fergus to one side, Brother Benedict herded the Jews from the sacristy, cattle prod in hand, out through the fountained cloister where gargoyles spouted mocking tongues of ice, and into the outer court, where the furious townsfolk waited for their prey.

"SWINDLERS, FRAUDSTERS, HEATHENS!" they chanted, as bailiffs and burgesses, peasants and paupers, fell upon the unarmed moneylenders, pelting the screaming women and children with stones and sharp flints. "Death to the filthy usurers!" they shrieked, as the first victim swayed and fell.

Brother Fergus opened his eyes with a shudder. He would remember the scene for the rest of his life, from the flinging of the first sharp stone, to the image of old Eli Abrahams, tears streaming down his face, cradling his dead wife in his arms.

"Not Benedict!" muttered Brother Fergus bitterly as he plunged blindly down the steps of *The Frisky Friar* with Mungo at his heels. "That murderer must never be abbot of Saint Wilfred's. Not as long as I have breath in this body!"

As Brother Fergus rounded the corner of Fleshmonger

Street and into Jewry Lane, he almost collided with a tall hooded figure. The shadowy form shrank into the darkness, head bowed, and let him pass. He waited without moving until the sacrist and his rangy dog were out of sight, and then ducked furtively down the alleyway beside the stone house of Eli Abrahams. He glanced warily over his shoulder to check that he was unobserved, then knocked very softly on the moneylender's door.

Chapter 8

The Moneylender

Eli Abrahams wearily pulled off his fringed prayer shawl and rolled the holy scroll into its silken cover. His lean grey face had once been handsome – before grief had hunched his tall spare frame, and streaked his ebony beard with silver. He jumped at the soft knock on the yard door. *Abigail's been quick with the ale,* he thought, with a stab of guilty regret. He had meant to play his Jew's-harp for a while – feel its magical essence vibrating in his fingers – spend some time alone after the business of the day. Abigail was a good daughter, but sometimes he needed time by himself – time to remember Miriam.

He removed his prayer cap and took a candle from the table, fumbling for the iron key. He hadn't always locked up at night – but times were crueller now. There was a new tiled roof where the vulnerable thatch had been – and a stronger, sturdier door.

"You took your time, moneylender," hissed the hooded form as it ducked under the dripping lintel.

"I was not expecting company," replied Eli irritably, locking the door behind the visitor. "I thought you were the ale jug," he muttered to himself. The shadow of his beard preceded his candle down the short, low passage to the counting room. "It is late for business."

"But you would not turn business away, I think," returned the cloaked figure coldly, placing a hessian sack on the table with a promising thud.

"That would depend on its nature, my friend," said Eli carefully, eyeing the bag. "Your visits are becoming more frequent. Your debt is increasing …"

"And a high price you charge for the privilege, moneylender!" snapped the stranger. "You still have the goods I have placed in pledge. You have the sealed bonds. As long as the goods are redeemed …"

Eli Abrahams snorted in disgust. "A high price is necessary, my friend, since the craft guilds close their doors to those of my faith. No other profession is open to us. And even money lending has now become precarious, since you Christians have dreamed up new ways to settle old debts. I live in constant fear of a long knife in the dark."

The moneylender thrust his arm inside the mysterious bundle and pulled out a golden altarpiece, turning the beautiful object, so that it gleamed in the flickering candlelight.

"So what will you give me, extortioner?" said the stranger, impatient to be gone. "Make haste and name your price or I will take my business elsewhere."

"But *'elsewhere'* might ask more questions," replied Eli calmly, weighing the note of desperation in his visitor's voice. He drew a fist of coins from his leather money pouch and placed them, clinking, on the table. "The wise moneylender has neither eyes nor ears, as my old father used to say. I do not question who you are, but I know full well where this treasure comes from, and I must deduct the price of my silence from the loan."

"Father!" A soft voice from the other side of the wattle shutter. "Hurry and open the door – my feet are wet."

The cloaked figure glanced furiously from the small pile of coins on the table to the window and back again. "But this cannot represent the ornament's full value," he spat.

"My people owe you Christians nothing. This is a business transaction – that is all. Your seal on this wax tablet, if you please, or I will save my gold for another more desperate than yourself," hissed Eli, hurriedly softening the wax in the candle flame. "One moment, my dear," he called to Abigail through the shutter. "I am removing my prayer shawl."

For the beat of a pulse, Eli thought his caller would turn to leave, taking the ornament with him. But then, with a groan of disgust mingled with despair, he pressed his seal into the soft wax, frantically raking the gold coins across the table with his free hand.

Eli nodded in satisfaction. "You may be assured of my discretion, my friend," he smiled frostily, moving towards the front door. "I assume you wish to leave through the back."

"What kept you, Father?" grumbled Abigail, unlacing

her overshoes. "It's as slippery as hog's grease out there. There's talk in the Frisky Friar of flattened corn, and on the eve of the Lammas Day Fair too." She frowned at the dark footprints on the floor of the small hall. "Company?"

"Just business, Abbi," said her father, in guarded tones. "Another spendthrift Christian – desperate for a loan."

"Well it's late for visitors, Father," she scolded, pouring ale into a pewter tankard. "I've told you not to open the door when I'm out. *The Frisky Friar* is full of strangers tonight. And there's grave news from the abbey, too. The abbot is dead. Bessie Miller told me."

Eli Abrahams shrugged. "Well I'll not shed a tear for him, Abigail," he wheezed, lowering himself stiffly into a chair and pulling a woollen shawl about his shoulders. "He was never a man of God."

"The Brothers were talking about who's to be the new abbot ..."

"And that is no concern of ours either, Abigail," he reproved, as a fit of coughing seized his thin frame, "and anyway, I thought I had told you not ... to fraternise with ... Bessie Miller." Eli sank back in the chair, exhausted. Abigail noticed with a pang how thin his face had grown, his lips narrower than ever.

"Hush Father," she urged, pulling his shawl more tightly around him. "You know very well that Bessie's my friend, despite our different faiths. You're making yourself ill with bitterness and grief."

"She's a Gentile, my dear," he reproved. "We can never be friends. You spend too much time up at Tirley Grange Mill."

Abigail turned with a pout and tossed some thyme into the rabbit stew that was bubbling over the hearth. "Bessie and I have things in common, Father. I'm an outsider – and so is she in a way. Don't forget, her mother was Alice de Lacy before she married Gabriel Miller. The peasants say she gives herself airs … especially the girls … but that's just bitter herbs, because she's so pretty."

Eli Abrahams smiled tenderly. His clever daughter might be able to read like the miller's girl but they were as different as apples and onions – one so plump and comely and the other, small for her age with hair as straight as the crow flies.

Abigail stuck out her chin. "There's good and bad in all faiths, Father. And talking of the hated Gentiles," she added with a spark of mischief, "I saw Brother Fergus at the Frisky Friar …"

Her father shifted uneasily, sensing defeat. "Yes well, Abigail, you see … there's good and bad …"

"…in all faiths," they finished together with a laugh.

"So at least we agree on something," said Abigail, "and if I'm not mistaken – that rabbit stew smells ready to eat."

Lammas Day –
August 1st 1220

Chapter 9

The Wheel of Fire

The next day was Lammas Day, the celebration of the first fruits of the harvest, and the morning sky was as blue as a heron's egg. Alice Miller lifted the huge wheel of Lammas bread from the oven in the stifling kitchen of Tirley Grange and held it up for her husband to admire. "It will look well on the altar tomorrow, won't it Bessie?" she said, turning to her daughter.

Bessie was busy, scratching away with a goose quill on a tiny piece of parchment. She glanced up distractedly as she poked the charm into the centre of a shiny fortune loaf.

"What a little sorceress you are," teased Gabriel, squinting at one of the scraps of writing. *"To be sure to meet your heart's desire,"* he read, *"dance around the wheel of fire."*

"Give that back, Father," squealed Bessie, reddening. "You try and think of fifty different things to write."

"Oh leave her be, Gabriel," chided Alice, pushing back a

strand of fair hair with a floury hand. "She's doing a grand job there."

"Well, I'll be off down to Saint Wilfred's with the hand cart if I'm not wanted here," said Gabriel, smoothing Bessie's mop of black hair. "Old Brother Silas asked to borrow it to take his remedies to the market square." The red-faced miller fingered the top of his head gently. "He tells me he has a new cure for baldness ..."

"Let me take the cart down to the monastery for you, Father," cried Bessie, jumping up with a fortune bun in her hand. "I've nearly finished these."

Her parents exchanged uneasy glances. "I ... I don't think so Bessie, thank you all the same," hesitated Gabriel. "Er, the fact is, Prior Solomon had a word in my ear – only yesterday as it happens. He thinks you're too old to be running so free at the monastery ... now you're ..."

"... almost a woman," finished Alice gently. "It's not fair on the older novices," she explained, intercepting Gabriel's grateful glance with a smile, "you being so bonny and all."

Bessie sat down slowly, an arrow of hurt between her black brows as Gabriel deftly changed the subject. "I'm surprised old Brother Silas is going to the Lammas Fair today, what with Abbot Theodore hardly cold in the chapel."

Alice nodded, pursing her lips in disapproval. "It doesn't seem right to me either, God rest his soul. But then some do say Brother Silas has sold his soul to the Devil," she added with a shudder. "Margery Cheeseman saw him with a black dog up by the weir the other night."

Gabriel groaned as he bent over his bootlaces. "Before or after her flagon of ale?" he scoffed. "Leastways, Brother

Silas won't be the only monk at the fair, you mark my words. If there's a penny to be made, that fat bursar will be watching out for it."

"Brother Benedict is planning elephant rides. Tom told me," said Bessie. "I mean, *Brother Thomas*," she added, with a demure glance at her father, as she placed the last charm bun casually on the top of the golden pile.

The voice of Abigail Abrahams floated through the open door on a stream of spicy air. "I helped myself to the eggs if you don't mind, Mistress Miller," she called. "I knew you'd be busy and Father wants me safe home before the barley beer starts flowing."

"Oh, Abbi, won't you come to the Lammas Fair with me?" begged Bessie, pulling her into the kitchen. "I'll bind gillyflowers in your hair ..."

Abigail pushed her friend away with a brief shake of her head. "You know Father wouldn't let me Bessie, and anyway, I'd feel a fool with flowers in my straight hair, especially ..." She paused.

Bessie's mother gave the grape jelly a more vigorous stir. "Especially what, Abigail?" she said. "Not everyone hates you and your kind you know. There's a good many people who feel ashamed of what happened last winter. You're inside too much, Abbi. Look at Bessie – as brown as a Lammas loaf. You could look at the stalls with us – and there's a rope dancer all the way from Arabia ... and a juggling bear."

Abigail shook her head, an uneasy smile on her lips. "I know you mean to be kind Mistress Alice, but I'm wary of the town at the best of times, and you know what happens to people when the ale's flowing free."

Bessie screwed up her lips, but she knew Abbi was right. "Well at least you can take a fortune bun home with you," she said, "even if you don't feel like dancing around the wheel of fire with me tonight."

The market cross was garlanded with oak leaves and the doors of the town houses were decorated with flowers and stalks of wheat. Brother Silas trundled the miller's handcart across the beaten earth of the square, swathed in a thick grey mantle in spite of the sizzling day.

"You must be hot, Brother Physician," said Brother Benedict, striding past, leading his elephant by a silken halter. He had rolled up the sleeves of his habit to the elbows, revealing the flaccid red meat of his arms.

The physician shivered. "I am of a phlegmatic humour, Brother Bursar – my element is water. Cool and placid – unlike yourself," he added, his spite thinly veiled.

The bursar's eyes bulged. "Your meaning, exactly?" he snapped.

"You are choleric, my dear bursar," returned the physician. "Fire element – hot tempered and peevish. My exact opposite," he added with an icy smile, turning away from the bursar and uncurling his tattered list of remedies. "Now, let me see: mole's blood for freckles, frog's spittle for warts, ants' eggs for colds, goose grease for chests ..."

"I hadn't thought to see you here," persisted the bursar. "One might have thought a physician's place was in the abbey at a time like this. Our dear abbot is hardly cold in the chapel."

Brother Silas shivered, as if in sympathy with the temperature of the dead abbot. "And what, pray, can I be expected to do with a corpse, Brother Bursar? Some do say that I am a necromancer, a raiser of the dead. But I assure you, I can be of infinitely more use to the living than to those who have departed this life!"

Brother Benedict lumbered off, keeping in step with the swaying elephant. Brother Silas followed the clumsy form with his eyes. *Placid I may be, my fat friend,* Silas thought bitterly, *but we of a phlegmatic humour can be deeply unforgiving too.* He slammed a jar of ground woodlice down on his stall, making the other pots rattle to attention. He'd heard the spiteful rumours about his part in Abbot Theodore's death – and he didn't have to look further than the bursar to discover their origins.

The sun rose higher in the turquoise sky, intense heat burning down on the market square with its crush of carts and booths heaped high with yellow honey and beeswax candles, trinkets and ribbons.

"That's one silver penny if you please," said Bessie, handing a fortune bun to a neighbour. "I hope it all comes true for you." She narrowed her eyes, scanning the bustling market square for the hundredth time looking for Tom, but novices were as scarce as hedgehogs in winter. She tidied her stall despondently, placing the bun marked with a cross at the back. She'd made it especially for Tom – spiked with her finest charm.

As Bessie was selling her fortune buns, Tom was chewing his quill into a bedraggled pulp in the novices' day room. He gazed blankly at his page with its title scrawled untidily at the top: *Death and the Day of Judgement.* Below the heading was a mess of blots and crossings out. He couldn't even think of a first sentence. Brother Odo was scribbling away as if he was in a writing race, his left hand stuck up in the air, waving frantically for more parchment. Tom craned his neck to see what Herbert had written but Herbert's head was slumped on his script, his abandoned quill trembling to the rhythm of his gentle snores.

"Brother Dunstan," called Felix, jumping up, his hand in the air. "Tom's trying to copy from Herbert!"

Tom froze as Brother Dunstan slammed down his book, *On Deceit and Disobedience: A Novice Master's Guide to Discipline,* an indignant glare in his heavy lidded eyes. As he scraped back his stool, his fingers twitched indecisively above a selection of canes on his desk, each handle carved with one of the seven deadly sins. "Hmmm," he mused, a malicious smile on his face. *English elm for envy, a whip of willow for wrath, a cane of poplar for pride.* "The larch lash for laziness I think," he murmured as he rose slowly to his feet and began to approach Tom's desk, his knuckles white around the switch. Tom's palms were sweating as he slid his hands under the desk.

Suddenly the door rattled open. "Er … sorry to interrupt Brother Dunstan. Prior Solomon wants you in his study," said an apologetic monk.

The transformation was instant. Brother Dunstan's mean lips relaxed, like a purse when the string is released. His cane clattered to the floor. His mouth opened and closed – eager as a mouse trap. "P…Prior Solomon wants me?" he stammered, writhing in ecstasy. "I must go at once! Tell Prior Solomon I'm … er…er… I'm coming right away," he gabbled, darting for the door without a backward glance. "Now remember," he called breathlessly over his shoulder. "If I find any of you have sneaked off to the Lammas Fair – there'll be the Devil to pay!" And he whirled out of the room, almost tripping over his own feet in his fluster to arrive at the prior's study before he'd even had time to set off.

Tom poked Herbert hard in the ribs. "Come on you lazy lump. Wake up! It seems our luck has changed."

The day was drawing to its close and the swifts were flying high in the sky on the balmy draughts of dusky air when Bessie finally spotted Tom. *He's here after all!* she thought, with a hurt frown. *Why didn't he come and find me?* Tom was lounging against a hay bale with a group of novices, a twisted crown of periwinkle on his head at a jaunty angle, drowning his sorrows in a tankard of barley beer. They'd escaped from Brother Dunstan in high spirits, only to arrive at the fair to see *The Singing Sisters* from Saint Hilda's carrying off the ballad prize that should have been rightly theirs.

Bessie strolled up to him, swallowing her pride. "Come on, Tom," she called casually. "Aren't you going to watch the fire wheel? Why don't you give the farm lads a hand to roll it up Barley Hill?"

"Come on Tom!" mimicked a couple of novices, grinning at each other. Tom felt his cheeks flame. He pretended he hadn't heard her.

"Get up, Herbert," he urged, pulling at his friend's robe to cover his blushes. "Surely you've eaten enough honey apples for one day."

Now Bessie's pride was really stung. She stared hard at Tom. What could be the matter? He looked just the same as he always did except he had a spot on his chin … and there was a dark shadow on his top lip.

"Let's show those farm boys what we can do," cried Tom much too loudly, avoiding the hurt in her eyes. He felt ashamed of himself, but he knew why the boys were laughing.

The novices took turns with the ploughboys to roll the great tar covered wheel to the top of the hill, hands black with sticky tar, the sweaty townsfolk surging after, faces grotesque in the flaming torchlight. The wheelwright stepped forward and held a flaming brand to the gluey pitch around its rim as he intoned the Lammastide song:

> *Turn, turn, wheel of fire!*
> *The days grow short, the corn grows higher*
> *Thresh the grain, blow chaff away*
> *God bless us all this Lammas Day!*

Slowly, slowly the flames began to flicker around the circle of tar until at the last possible moment he let it go, and then it was rolling, spinning like Saint Catherine's wheel, back down the hill again. Cheering peasants raced it down, following the lurching golden hoop, bronze sparks bright against the indigo sky. Gathering speed, it careered towards the river bank until it tumbled, fizzing into the water, followed by the sticky boys, who plunged in after it to wash the thick black tar from their hands. Nobody noticed the dark shadow of Brother Benedict striding past with the elephant, his leather purse fat with silver.

Chapter 10

The Harvest Moon

The harvest moon was as round as a Lammas loaf. Its cold silver light rippled on the water as Tom and his friends straggled in sombre silence along the bright line of the River Twist towards Saint Wilfred's. Tom was in low spirits. The golden glow of barley beer was wearing off – and he didn't want to go back to the abbey. There'd been an ominous atmosphere ever since Abbot Theodore's death – a prickly tension in the air. The Lammas fair had distracted him for an hour or two but his dark mood returned to haunt him, wrapping itself around him like a gloomy cloak. He had never wanted to be a novice in the first place, but it was just about bearable with Abbot Theodore in charge. But who would be the next abbot? And how would life change if it was Prior Solomon?

"We'll be in serious trouble from Brother Dunstan when we get back," said Tom miserably, "and it wasn't even worth it. I didn't enjoy the fair."

"Bessie gave me a fortune bun," said Ed brightly, trying to lighten the gloom.

Tom gave a small smile. "What does it say? Prepare to become abbot of Saint Wilfred's?" he teased.

"*Pride goes before a fall!*" lisped the little novice, wrinkling his nose. "I don't understand it at all."

Tom scowled. "Well that's a dreary one, Ed."

Tom could have done without the reminder of Bessie. As if he didn't have worries enough. *Why was I so mean to her?* he asked himself. But he knew the answer, and he was ashamed of it. He hadn't wanted to lose face with his friends.

"Keep up, Herbert," he called, glancing back over his shoulder. "Brother Dunstan's bound to have missed us by now. What's the betting he's locked the gates?"

They were approaching the crossroads where a desolate skeleton creaked in an iron cage on a gibbet, its shirt in tatters and its boots still on. Tom shuddered, shrinking away.

"Why don't they cut him down?" said Ed in a shaky voice.

"He's an example, Ed," grimaced Tom. "A kind of warning to everyone else …"

There was a sudden high pitched squeak and a rush of black wings so close to Tom's face that he felt his hair lift. He jumped back with a cry but it was only a bat, hunting a night-flying beetle. The boys quickened their pace, scuttling past the gallows in gloomy silence, their eyes fixed on the ground. Tom thought how loud their sandals sounded, scrunching along the dry earth track. He tried in vain to think of something cheerful to raise their spirits but for once even Tom was short of a joke.

As Tom had predicted, the north gate was locked, so they crossed the rickety bridge and came up through the murky shadows of the apple orchard, feet slithering on the rotting windfalls scattered on the ground. Little Ed drew closer to Tom as they skirted the beast house with its putrid smell of dung and decay. Odd how somewhere familiar by day could seem so eerie by night. Tom could hear the soft thump of the animals in the stalls, settling down for the night. The sound should have been comforting but for some reason it made him more anxious. The night air had a chilly edge, chasing the last fumes of barley beer away.

"I don't like it here," said Ed in a tight voice. "Can't we go round and knock on the north gate?"

Tom forced a laugh. "Don't be silly. And wake Brother Dunst…" He paused, his face half in shadow half in lantern light.

"What's wrong?" said Herbert.

"I … I thought I heard something," said Tom, his heart missing a beat. "Listen, there it is again …"

Herbert stepped up softly behind. "It sounds like someone groaning," he whispered, an icy finger of fear tracing a line down his back.

The moaning came again, weaker now, faint but unmistakeably human, followed by a long, low growl.

"What the devil …?" gasped Tom, springing into a run. "Quick, follow with the lantern, Herbert!" he cried, racing towards the lioness's cage. He crashed past the offal bucket, ripping his habit on the pump handle as he tore across the beast house yard. Reaching the cage, he clutched the cold iron bars with both hands and peered into the darkness.

Herbert limped up with the lantern, clutching his shin. "Not so fast, Tom! Hold the lamp – I've cut myself ..." He stopped suddenly, appalled by the expression on Tom's face. "God in heaven! What is it? What the devil's the matter, you look ..."

"It's B ... B ...Brother Benedict," gasped Tom, clapping his hand to his mouth. "At least ... that's his purse on the ground." Herbert could see the whites of Tom's eyes, glistening in the lantern light. He dragged his gaze from Tom's face, willing himself to be brave, steeling himself to dare to look beyond the cold bars and into the lion's cage. Herbert's lips were moving – mouthing a silent prayer as he forced his eyes to focus on the hunched form of Delilah, crouching in her cage, her yellow eyes gleaming.

"It's ... it's ... horrible ..." Tom managed to whimper, before bending and vomiting over his sandals.

"Oh, my God," whispered Herbert, his eyes transfixed by the bloody bundle of mangled flesh that had once been Brother Benedict. The body lay still now. No human sound came from the cage – only the noise of tearing sinew as the lioness consumed her freshly killed supper; only the slick lapping of her rough tongue, as Delilah licked the bursar's sticky blood from her lips.

Herbert turned quickly at the sound of a footfall. "Don't look Ed!" he shouted, grabbing him roughly by the shoulders and spinning him round so that Ed couldn't see the gruesome scene. "Run and find the prior! Qu ...quick, g ...go now," he stammered, thrusting him away from the cage. "Tell him ... tell him there's been a ... an accident!"

Tom straightened up, wiping his mouth on his sleeve. "Accident?" he said grimly, pulling at the unyielding bars. "Don't you see, Herbert? This cage is locked ... but the key is on the *outside!* You can call it an accident if you like – but I'd call it murder!"

Chapter 11

Silver Pins

A bigail Abrahams woke with a start, her body drenched in sweat. Lights flickered across the thin window panes of polished horn – most likely the last merrymakers from the Lammas Fair rolling home with their bellies full of beer. It must be after midnight, she thought, noticing her tallow candle guttering to its death in a pool of mutton fat. She sat up, fingers raking her tangled hair.

How odd. There seemed to be a light in the front parlour, spilling into the passage outside her door. *Father must have left a lamp burning*, she thought, swinging her pale legs out of bed and groping with her toes for her new silk slippers – a present from Bessie on the way home from the fair. She could hear the low grumble of Eli's snoring as she crossed the passage. "He's so forgetful these days," she muttered, stopping on the parlour threshold with a puzzled frown. The house lamps were cold. The light in the passage was coming from the street outside – fiery torchlight flickering on the walls.

She knew instinctively that something was wrong. A familiar cold prickle of fear crept through her body like icy water at the soft sound of shuffling feet on dry earth. Dark shapes passed across the window. Her eyes followed them, ears straining to catch the meaning of the ominous rise and fall of voices. Abigail caught her breath as the iron latch of the street door began to clack up and down, worked by an unseen hand.

Abbi wanted to scream but the muscles had formed a tight knot in her throat and fear kept her rooted to the spot. Her mind was spinning. *We have a strong lock and a sturdy new door* she told herself, but even as she stared, she knew in her heart there was no escape.

There was a scuffle of feet. A rabble of voices. Groans as if someone were shouldering a heavy weight. A dull thud … and then another … followed by an ear splitting crash like a giant's hammer. The door shivered on its hinges. Abbi watched with rising panic as the planks began to strain apart, her body quivering with tension. She half turned as Eli stumbled sleepily into the parlour, roused by the sudden noise, his woollen shawl clutched round his bony shoulders.

Then all at once everything exploded in splinters of sound and light. The sturdy door of the moneylender's house was no match for a thick oak trunk in the hands of drunkards, intent upon a hue and cry. With a scream of splitting wood the door burst inwards and the ale sodden mob roared in, lips drawn back, faces blood red in the flaring torchlight.

"Where's the Jew? Where's the vicious murderer?"

"The yard door," cried Eli. "Come on Abbi! Follow me – then run!"

But it was too late. "He's here, the villain's here!" roared the town constable, seizing the frail old man and wrestling him needlessly to the ground.

"No!" screamed Abigail. She snatched up the nine-branched candelabra, rushing at the bearded men who were circling Eli on the ground like thugs at a bear baiting, cursing and beating him with cudgels. "He's a sick old man … have pity …"

"Take that, you murdering Jew! If you don't come quietly we'll burn your house down!"

"Stop, stop for pity's sake!" sobbed Abigail, dragging at their jerkins, tears streaming down her cheeks. "What do you mean? What murder? What has my father done?"

"Don't give us them lies, Jewess!" snarled the constable, in a blast of alcoholic breath. "The news is all over the town." He grabbed her wrist and tried to wrest the weapon from her hand. "Brother Benedict's dead and we all know who killed him!"

Abigail sank her sharp teeth into his hand. He screamed and grabbed her by the hair but she twisted out of his grasp still clutching the candlestick. And then a well placed leg tripped her up and she crumpled to the floor like a fairground puppet.

"Run, Abbi! Run for help," groaned Eli, his face in the dirt. "Run for your life!"

Abigail retched with pain as she tried to drag herself across the floor, hearing the muffled sobs of her father as they pulled a hessian sack over his head. She screamed in helpless anguish as she watched them bind his hands and feet, but the thugs paid no heed to her cries.

"Hey! Come and look in 'ere," roared a voice from down the corridor. "There's chests full of jewels and golden caskets …"

"Now if this ain't my mum's old wedding band …" slurred a beery oaf, staggering into the front parlour holding a massive gold ring that could have belonged to the Pope himself.

"Now lads," barked the constable. "I'm in charge 'ere … no pillaging until …" His eyes bulged at the sight of a huge golden chalice.

"There's chests of the stuff … silver cups and candlesticks … altar crosses. And I'd swear by Saint Wilfred's bunion – this stuff comes from the abbey!"

Bessie Miller was too miserable to sleep. Why had Tom snubbed her at the Lammas Fair? She sat in the window seat of her garret room at Tirley Grange in her linen shift, listening to the tumbling sound of the River Twist splashing through the mill wheel, her hair still plaited with daisies and her mouth full of silver pins. Her blue dress lay in a crumpled heap covered in crumbs from a broken fortune bun. The harvest moon hung like a golden cheese over the great tithe barn, flooding her room with light, so she had no need of a candle to read the words of the incantation she'd bought from a peddler at the fair:

> *Weave the pins within your gown*
> *Light a candle; lay you down*

Put your hands behind your head
And dream all night of the boy you'll wed

Bessie was just fastening the last silver pin, when she heard a frantic crying in the yard below. She turned to the window with a start, stabbing her thumb and splattering her nightgown with blood.

"Heavens, Abbi! What's happened?" she gasped, leaning out over the lintel. In an instant she was racing to her chamber door. She groaned at the stiffness of the latch as she wrenched it open, flying to the top of the stairs to call to her father. But before she had time to draw breath, the door below burst open and Abigail Abrahams stumbled over the stone threshold, black hair wild, feet bare and bleeding, like a demon scarecrow.

"Father!" shrieked Bessie, "Father!" But Gabriel Miller was already on the narrow landing in his undershirt, an iron candlestick in hand. He stared, bewildered, at the sobbing form below. Abigail tried to speak but her words were incoherent, interspersed with gulping sobs. Gabriel Miller thrust the candle into Bessie's hand, scalding her wrist with molten wax as he bounded down the stairs two at a time, reaching Abigail just too late to catch her as she swayed and fell at his feet with a dull thud.

Part Two

The Wheel of Fortune
August 2nd 1220

Chapter 12

Owl Feathers

The town constable's head felt like a pig's bladder at the end of a game of football. He pressed his fingers to his temples with a groan and shook his head so that his flabby jowls wobbled from side to side, leaving the rest of his face behind.

"I should have stuck to good old English ale last night, Daniel," he moaned with a belch. "That fancy French stuff's given me a head like a split log."

"I don't feel too frisky meself," yawned his companion. "I feel like I've got a hedgehog in me throat."

The constable slapped the rump of a ragged little pony that stood patiently between the shafts of a hay cart. "Come on then. Let's get this lot up to the abbey – see what Prior Solomon has to say about it. Just look at it all – embroidered cloaks, gold and silver chalices, jewelled crosses. He'll be pleased to get this back, I'll be bound, and there might be a little something in it for me," he said, rubbing his thumb and fingers together.

"But who do you think has been pawning the abbey treasure?" said Daniel. "They're as rich as kings, them monks. They can't need no moneylenders. And talking of moneylenders – what did happen to the old Jew after I passed out?"

The constable hauled a hide cover over the treasure and roped it down. "Chained in the town lock up since you ask, and he can stay there 'til 'is feet rot off for all I care!"

Prior Solomon stared from his window across the narrow bend of the River Twist towards the beast house on the far bank, his finely arched lips pursed in an expression of distaste. He could just make out a mound of fresh straw in the outer enclosure of Delilah's cage on the spot where Brother Benedict's least edible parts had been discovered the night before. Two servants in short tunics stood guard at the entrance, gossiping with a group of novices. The prior clicked his tongue impatiently. The abbey was bristling with the news already, and the sun still low in the sky. He gave a start at a noise behind him.

"I trust you are still expecting me, Prior?" said Brother Silas, sidling into the study without a knock, the Caladrius perched on his arm. "I was afraid you might have forgotten our appointment in view of ..." He paused, his thin nostrils flaring and cast a disdainful glance in the direction of a bronze incense burner in the shape of a Persian cat. The room was thick with frankincense.

The prior turned slowly from the window, with a fastidious twist of his mouth. *Brother Silas always smelt of sulphur.* The Caladrius glared maliciously from the physician's glove but if Prior Solomon was disturbed by the bird, he gave no sign. "And what, pray, is that creature doing on your arm?" he asked, with an upward tilt of his nose.

"I rescued it from the beast house just as soon as the glad tidings broke," replied Silas, a possessive hand on the bird's feathers. "It will now reside in the infirmary where it should have been lodged in the first place."

Prior Solomon raised an eyebrow and moved delicately upwind of Brother Silas, nearer to the incense burner. "You surely do not mean to imply that you are pleased that a fellow monk has been savaged by a lion?"

"I *imply* nothing, Prior," retorted the physician, unrolling a star chart and settling the Caladrius at one end of it and an ornamental inkwell at the other. "I say it plainly. I am *glad* the fat bursar is dead – and I believe I speak for more than myself when I say it! But happily, it is not my job to discover the culprit."

Prior Solomon inclined his head. "I was informed by the local constable last night that we daily expect the King's Justices from Westminster for the autumn assizes," he said gravely. "A happy coincidence in view of the regrettable incident here last night." He sighed. "As if we were not in turmoil enough already with the death of Abbot Theodore ..."

Brother Silas sniffed. "And the elections for the new abbot are infinitely more interesting than the trivial matter of who turned the key in the beast house lock!" he retorted rudely. "Now, would you care to see your horoscope?" he asked, sliding a sly yellow thumb over the doodle of his own name in the margin of the chart.

There was a tentative knock on the door. Brother Dunstan, poked his head around the frame, his earnest face like a waxy cheese. "I am sorry to intrude at such a troubled time, Prior Solomon," grovelled the novice master. "But the town constable is in the outer court. He says he's brought something important," he added wringing his hands unctuously. "Something you need to see before anyone else."

The shrill voices of the novices floated through the arched Quillery window into the outer court of the abbey. The gruesome news had spread like the sweating sickness and Brother Ambrose, the quill master, was struggling to keep control. He was more than a little put out. He had been looking forward to this morning's *Presentation of the New Quills,* but the boys could talk of little else except the murder in the beast house and didn't seem to care whether their new quill pen was the flight feather of a Silver Pheasant or a Whistling Duck.

"Just his sandals left ..." whispered a fiery haired novice, rolling his eyes with relish.

"And the buckle of his belt, I was told ..."

"Boys, boys, boys!" pleaded Brother Ambrose. The old monk's face was as pink as a baby. Two plumes of feathery hair, like cygnet down, sprouted from each ear. "I think a Little Owl quill would be just the right size for young Edmund ... Good Heavens! What's the rumpus now?"

There was a commotion in the outer court. The novices raced to the arched window at the far end of the quillery, tumbling over each other in their haste to clamber out. A heavily laden hay cart stood by the north gate, the town constable standing guard beside it, brimming with self-importance.

"Hands off, you thieving ruffians," he barked, as a motley crowd of rat catchers and stable boys, laundry maids and novices gathered round.

Prior Solomon was standing aloof, eyeing the cart suspiciously and trying to ignore Brother Dunstan who was bobbing at his elbow, almost treading on the prior's toes in his eagerness to be near him.

"So Constable," said the prior stiffly. "Am I to understand that you have arrested Eli Abrahams, the moneylender, for the murder of Brother Benedict? May I enquire how you discovered the culprit so quickly?"

The constable's face was smug. "We don't waste no time when we've got a vicious killer to catch. It was only a matter of time before one of them Jews took 'is revenge on the bursar for what happened last winter. It won't be long before we're stretching that heathen neck on the gallows! But that's not what we're 'ere for right now. You just take a look at what we found at the old swindler's house. I'll wager you can't guess, eh prior?" he said with a familiar nudge in the prior's ribs.

Prior Solomon peered down his long nose, as if the constable were vermin dropped at his feet by a dog.

"Well, hurry up man," snapped Brother Dunstan impatiently, as the constable began to untie the ropes that held the tarpaulin. "Prior Solomon is a busy man. Anyone would think he had all day to stand around talking."

A dairymaid squealed. The blacksmith's boy gasped and everyone surged forward like a flock of sheep with the dog behind them. They stared in wonder at the mounds of gold and silver, jewels and fine embroidered vestments winking in the sun.

"Well, Prior?" said the constable triumphantly. "What d'ya say now?"

Prior Solomon's face paled. Brother Dunstan glanced at him slyly, lacing his fingers together with an ingratiating stoop. "Do correct me if I'm wrong, Prior Solomon, but this looks remarkably like the sacristy treasure." He pursed his prim lips into a mean pink line. "Far be it from me to accuse a fellow monk but I fear *Brother Fergus* is the only person in Saint Wilfred's Abbey who is in possession of a key."

Brother Fergus was deep in conversation with Brother Ethelwig when his attention was attracted by the rumpus in the outer court. He was finding it hard to shake off a feeling of well-being, in spite of the shocking tragedy of Brother Benedict's death in the beast house. Why should he feign emotion that he did not feel? He stepped from the cloister humming a new ballad, through the cellarer's cool parlour and out into the sunshine, winking at Tom as he caught sight of him in the crowd.

He stopped suddenly, his face a confusion of bewilderment and disbelief. The entire contents of the sacristy, his sole responsibility, lay piled in a hay cart, the town constable standing guard, swollen up like a puff adder. Brother Fergus's hand flew instinctively to his waist, his fingers groping for the heavy sacristy key, with its fob in the shape of a chalice.

Everyone was staring at the sacrist. His face changed colour, from scarlet to white and back to scarlet again. Prior Solomon stepped forward, a tic of anger twitching at the corner of his eye. "Take Brother Fergus to the abbey lock-up," he commanded, with a contemptuous twist of his mouth. "It appears we have a thief in our midst!"

The abbey bell clanged out, calling the monks to dinner – but no one moved. Then suddenly the silence was broken. Little Edmund, the youngest novice of all, fell to the ground in a dead faint, his owl feather quill spiralling down and landing in the dust by his side.

Chapter 13

A Fishy Letter

The refectory faced south over the River Twist, a lofty chamber with soaring windows, thick pillars and wide vaulting arches. A stone balcony dominated the room, and Brother Odo was already standing at the eagle lectern, leafing through the vellum bound Bible, making a noisy display of finding the right place.

The novices filed in from the cloisters and stood whispering behind their benches at the bottom of the hall. Tom's face was dark with fury. He couldn't believe what had just happened in front of his eyes. *How dare Prior Solomon send Fergus to the abbey lock-up, his hands shackled like a common sheep stealer? Brother Fergus of all people – the best monk in the abbey!* The senior monks entered last. Tom shot Brother Dunstan a poisonous look as he scurried by, close on Prior Solomon's heels. Brother Ethelwig hobbled behind looking shocked and leaning on the quill master's sympathetic arm.

Brother Silas brought up the rear, submerged in a red flannel muffler.

Three places were vacant at the top table. There was, of course, no knife, spoon and pewter trencher for Abbot Theodore and Brother Benedict, but a space had been laid for Brother Fergus, and Ethelwig stood mournfully next to the empty trencher.

"My Brethren!" proclaimed Prior Solomon, surveying the tense faces of the senior monks. "The Angel of Death is truly in our midst! By now you will all know of the horrifying death of Brother Benedict, mauled in the beast house by his own lion. This is all the more shocking, coming as it does only a day after the passing of our beloved leader, Abbot Theodore, who will be buried after Prime tomorrow ..."

Tom swallowed hard. *Was it only last night?* So much had happened in between. He closed his eyes as the memories flooded in – the groaning in the darkness ... the body ... the blood ... and Delilah, licking her lips. He was only dimly aware of the rise and fall of Prior Solomon's voice in the silent hall:

"The villain responsible has been apprehended ... the moneylender Eli Abrahams ... the shameful matter of the sacristy treasure ... Brother Fergus ... punished by the church court in London ..."

Tom jumped at the sound of his friend's name. Prior Solomon was wiping his brow with the napkin that covered his trencher. It had all been too much, even for the level-headed prior. *"And until such time,"* concluded Prior Solomon, with evident relief, *"all gossip must immediately cease. Now let us say grace."*

But Prior Solomon had wasted his breath. Down on the novices' trestle, rumour and speculation had exploded again.

"How can they be sure it was Brother Fergus who stole the sacristy treasure?" blurted Tom furiously, banging his fist on the table. "How dare Brother Dunstan accuse him like that? He'd say anything to suck up to Prior Solomon!"

Herbert was ladling the thick vegetable broth from a basin. Tom snatched a brimming bowl from his hand, clumsily slopping the contents on the table. "Just because he holds the sacristy key doesn't mean he stole the contents of the cupboard."

"Oh doesn't it?" said Brother Felix in a sarcastic tone. "That's exactly what it does suggest, if you want my opinion. Of course, nobody would expect *you* to believe anything bad about your beloved Fergus," he sneered. "Anyway, I'd have thought that was the least of our worries. There's been a murder in case you'd forgotten."

Tom slammed down his spoon, splattering Felix with hot soup. "I'm hardly likely to forget," he said coldly, "since I was the one who discovered it."

"Are you feeling any better, Ed?" said Herbert, pointedly turning his back on Felix and plunging his knife into a bearded carp, fresh from the abbey pond. Edmund nodded, his eyes on the food. "Probably just the heat," he murmured.

"Well Brother Dunstan must be over the moon about Fergus," said Tom with an evil glare at Felix who was mopping his robe with a napkin. "He makes me sick, the way he oils up to the prior. Has anybody thought that with Fergus out of the way there'll be one less person to stand against Prior Solomon in the election? Pretty convenient as Fergus is one of the most popular monks at Saint Wilfred's. And with Brother Benedict dead, that's another one out of his precious prior's way!" Tom paused, a spoonful of pottage halfway to his mouth. He'd suddenly remembered Bessie. "Hey Herbert, you don't think the old moneylender really did murder Brother Benedict, do you?" he said anxiously. "Bessie will be beside herself. Abigail Abrahams is her best friend."

Herbert shrugged. "Don't ask me. There's any number of people who would happily have given Brother Benedict the evil eye. Job Pug, Brother Silas … Brother Fergus for that matter … even Bessie's father!"

"Don't say things like that," said Tom tartly. "Gabriel Miller was hardly going to murder the bursar because he'd put up the rent for the mill."

"Ouch, you're prickly today!" teased Herbert, pulling a fish bone out of his mouth. "Just because you fancy his daughter!"

Suddenly, a parchment dart landed in the middle of Tom's trencher. He spun round to look over his shoulder, just in time to see a halo of dark curls disappearing below the wide stone sill. *Bessie!* he grinned. He glanced around furtively to see if anyone else had noticed her. Herbert was still tucking into his carp. Tom wiped the sticky soup from the missile and lowered the note to his lap.

Tom

Have you heard the dreadful news? Eli

Abrahams has been arrested for the murder of Brother Benedict. Meet me in The Swallows' Nest as soon as you can.

Bessie

Chapter 14

The Swallows' Nest

"Keep going. Don't look back," whispered Tom, as he hustled Herbert through the arched opening that led from the refectory to the cloisters.

"Ouch!" squealed Herbert, as Tom's foot came down hard on his heel.

"Just *go!*" Tom hissed with a push. Prior Solomon had taken forever to dismiss them and now Tom could hear Brother Dunstan's shrill voice behind him, officiously recruiting novices to weed the graveyard. "Right turn and then dash for the warming room," he breathed down Herbert's neck. "We're wanted in the Swallows' Nest!"

Out in the cloisters, Tom broke into a run, slamming smack into Brother Ethelwig, who was emerging furtively from the kitchen with Job Pug by his side, carrying a trencher covered with a linen cloth. A loaf of bread shot from its hiding place and landed on the cobbles in an explosion of crusty crumbs.

"Er … just taking some food to Fergus er … to fill a corner until suppertime," stammered the old monk, glancing guiltily over his shoulder. "They're sure to let him out later – once the prior realises his mistake."

"So you think it's a mistake too?" said Herbert.

Ethelwig sniffed indignantly. "It's outrageous! Fergus was in *The Frisky Friar* after the fair last night – talking about polishing up the plate for when the Bishop comes for the election. Why would he do that if he knew the chalices had been pawned to the moneylender?" He nudged Job with his elbow. "You remember, don't you Job? In *The Frisky Friar* last night …"

"Er, yes sir," said Job, dusting down the blackened crust on the top of the loaf. "I remember …"

Ethelwig nodded briskly. "It must have been just at the time of the dreadful tragedy in the beast house, mustn't it Job?"

But Tom was hopping up and down in agitation, the note from Bessie scrunched in his hand. "Herbert, come *on*," he pleaded, pulling at his sleeve. "Tell Brother Fergus we don't believe he's a thief," he called, backing away from Ethelwig, and springing once more into a run as Brother Dunstan's voice drifted furiously through the refectory arch. "Come back … volunteers … to weed the cloisters …"

The boys slipped unseen into the warming room. "Quick, Herbert," urged Tom making straight for the great stone hearth. "Brother Dunstan's got a list as long as his new beard!"

The Swallows' Nest was a cosy rectangle of warm stone,

surrounded on three sides by a carved honey-coloured parapet and on the fourth by the grey slanting roof of the chapter house, entirely hidden from the cloisters down below. Tom had discovered it quite by chance last summer. He'd been surprised in the warming room one hungry afternoon, helping himself to one of the ripening cheeses that hung over the empty fireplace. At the sound of approaching footsteps, he'd escaped into the cold flue, worming his way up the blackened bricks, the stink of old soot in his nose and his mouth still crammed with cheese. He'd emerged with stinging eyes from the filthy chimney onto the fairytale roofscape of the abbey, bristling with pinnacles and gaping gargoyles, twisted spires and statues of saints. It had been their secret place ever since.

Now as the boys approached their den from above, they crouched down and dangled their sooty legs over the edge of a small roof, ready for the drop to the ferny balcony below. Tom landed with a thud, rolling over on the lichen that clung like yellow scabs to the stonework. Seconds later Herbert landed with a louder thud close by. But there was no sign of Bessie.

An ancient trunk of ivy as thick as a blacksmith's arm snaked up from the ground below, its huge hairy stem creeping up over the balustrade and branching away across the roof to the golden cross at the gable end of the chapter house. All of a sudden the ivy began to shudder and Bessie Miller tumbled over the parapet, her dress hitched up around her brown knees, her hair covered in broken twigs and her bare feet stained with moss.

"What on earth, Bessie …?" cried Tom. "Did you climb

up the ivy? You'll break your neck!" But he was secretly impressed.

Bessie glared at him. She was still smarting from his snubbing at the Lammas Fair. "How else am I supposed to come up?" she said sulkily. "I've been banished from the abbey! I'm not welcome anymore – Prior Solomon told Father – not that it would bother you these days. But never mind about that now ... did you get my note?"

The sun beat down on the Swallows' Nest as Bessie listened to the boys' part of the tale.

"...I'll never forget the sight as long as I live," finished Tom. "The pool of blood ... and the sound of Delilah ... licking her lips!"

Bessie's face was pale. "That's so disgusting," she breathed. "Don't tell me any more. I wouldn't ever be able to sleep at night again if I'd found the body. But I won't believe it was Eli Abrahams that locked him in!" she said defiantly. "He can't possibly have killed Brother Benedict. The constable and his gang don't care whether they've caught the right person or not. They hate the Jews and they'll take any excuse to hound them. They raised a hue and cry just as soon as the news broke last night. They threw him into the town gaol – but not until they'd beaten him up first."

Tom blew out his cheeks and let the air out slowly. "But how can you be so sure that it wasn't him? Old Eli certainly had a grudge against Brother Benedict. Everyone knows he blamed the bursar for the death of his wife."

Bessie clapped her hands to her ears. "How can you say that, Tom?" she cried. "He's a good man. Listen! They stayed in all day yesterday during the Lammas Fair and all evening. Abbi was with her father the whole time and she didn't even go out to *The Frisky Friar* for his usual jug of ale. I called in to give her a gift from the fair on my way to help the landlord at the inn, and Eli was already in his nightcap when I left their house in Jewry Lane!" She flung Tom a triumphant look.

"That's all very well," he said with a frown, "but why should the town constable look any further when they've found a scapegoat? As you say, nobody's interested in whether he's guilty or not. But there's something else, Bessie. Brother Fergus has been arrested. They found the entire contents of the sacristy treasure in Eli Abrahams's counting house. The prior's thrown Brother Fergus into the gaol below the latrines! They're sending him to London for trial ..."

Herbert was tearing an ivy leaf into tiny pieces. "This is all very odd – how everything's started to go wrong. Nothing ever happens at Saint Wilfred's and then suddenly Abbot Theodore dies. And then the next day Brother Benedict's horribly savaged in the beast house."

"Yes," said Tom grimly, "and in precisely the same way as little Obadiah Pug died. Talk about getting a taste of your own medicine. And then we find out that the sacristy treasure's been stolen ..."

"... and it turns up at Eli Abrahams' house – the very person they've arrested for the murder!" groaned Bessie, her voice rising again. "Father says the assizes are due any day now. The King's Justices could already be on their way, and we all know what they do with murderers!"

"Well, whoever was pawning the sacristy treasure will be delighted to have Eli Abrahams out of the way," said Tom. "He can't talk if he's hanged for murder!" Bessie stifled a choking sound. "You know," he continued, "I've a feeling there's a connection between all these events but I don't see what can it be."

Tom narrowed his eyes. It would be like searching for a thimble in a field of hay. There were so many people who hated Brother Benedict. Brother Silas for one – the bursar had accused him of poisoning Abbot Theodore. And then there was Brother Fergus! It was common knowledge that he hated Brother Benedict for the business with the Jews last winter. Tom's stomach dropped away as icy fingers of fear tightened round his heart. Not Brother Fergus! It was unthinkable! But Eli Abrahams had very good reason to wish the bursar dead, whatever Bessie might say. And then again – there was old Job Pug. Now *there* was a man with a motive…

"Well you're in a perfect position to investigate," came Bessie's voice, interrupting his reverie. "Who better? You're actually living on the spot. You can make enquiries – see if you can find something out. We must help Abbi. If Father's right and the Justices really are on their way, there's not a minute to lose."

The sun was dipping behind the chapter house roof and the shadow of a cross lay like a dark ruler over the warm stone of the Swallows' Nest.

"So are we all clear?" said Bessie. "Everyone's movements are suspicious until proved otherwise, including people we like such as Brother Ethelwig," she said firmly. "We can't allow friendship to cloud our judgement. Now, you know what you need to do, Tom? You must examine everything in the beast house right away."

He nodded. "We'll make a note of anything suspicious."

"Inside or outside Delilah's cage?" said Herbert in a grumpy voice. He was feeling a bit left out. Tom and Bessie were thick as treacle again, planning it all together.

"Don't be silly, Herbert," said Bessie impatiently, twisting her black hair into a thick plait. She turned back to Tom. "I'll persuade Abbi to visit Jewry Lane with me after curfew tonight and search Eli's ledgers. He's sure to have kept records. You never know – it might be relevant, and even if it isn't it could help to clear Brother Fergus's name. Now – I must get back to Tirley Grange before Abbi starts worrying. She's staying with us for a while. It's not safe for her in the town."

Tom prised off a crust of yellow lichen and shot it over the parapet with a determined flick. "So let's just sum up, Bessie. Eli Abrahams – he was with Abigail all evening."

Bessie nodded. "And Brother Fergus and Brother Ethelwig were in *The Frisky Friar* with me ..."

"*And* Job Pug," added Tom. "He was in *The Frisky Friar* with Ethelwig ..."

Bessie looked up sharply. "When? When was Job Pug in *The Frisky Friar?*"

"Last night with Ethelwig. Ethelwig told us they'd spent the evening in the inn together."

"Last night?" she frowned. "The night of the murder?" Bessie slowly shook her head. "Brother Fergus was there all right and Brother Ethelwig with him, but as for Job Pug – I didn't catch a glimpse of him all evening." She shrugged. "Like I said, everyone's a suspect until proved otherwise, and it sounds to me as if we've caught someone telling lies already!"

Chapter 15

The King's Justice

Sir Percy FitzNigel's fine silk leggings were fashionably tight around his well turned thighs; his hair the colour of ripe corn. A shirt of soft blue linen was caught up in a jewelled belt, drawn tight to display his slender waist, and on his head he wore the golden skull cap of a judge. His high pitched giggle had been known to shatter glass in the Palace of Westminster, and yet behind the frivolous mask his mouth was cruel and a spiteful glint gleamed in his hard green eye.

Sir Percy had just heard his last case of the day and he was in excellent mood. The case of Anna Blount and the poisoned hat had tickled him immensely. The old fishwife had gathered herbs on Midsummer's Eve and woven them into a bonnet for her friend, who after a day of blinding headaches had been found stone dead in the privy behind her hovel in Stinking Lane.

"Murder by Witchcraft!" he cried dismissively, scraping

back his stool. "Interrogate the prisoner with thumb screws!" He was in a furious rush. He didn't want to miss the afternoon hangings at Smithfield. If he hurried, he'd be just in time to see the culprits strung up on the three elms above the horse pond. Old Anna Blount was down on her knees, screaming for mercy, clawing at the sleeves of her gaolers, but Sir Percy kicked her casually aside and strode off down the hall towards the huge ribbed arch at the north end, without a backward glance.

"Hurry up, Fustian, you jaded jackdaw!" he called to his threadbare clerk who trotted along behind him like a mournful bloodhound.

"Have you no pity?" muttered Fustian underneath his breath.

"What did you say, you mumbling magpie?" snapped Sir Percy, rounding on him with an evil glare.

"Best lawyer in the city," cringed his clerk, shrinking down into his tattered gown.

Sir Percy looked unconvinced, but the air was so full of the screams of prisoners and the pleading of lawyers that he couldn't quite be sure. He picked his way gingerly through the rushes and sweet herbs that covered the floor of an immense hall. It was so large that three rowdy courts sat in session at once, the side aisles crammed with stalls selling striped law gowns, dusty books and the pens and parchment made by the monks of Westminster Abbey. Sir Percy held a linen cloth soaked in aniseed fastidiously to his nostrils, but not even this could disguise the evil stench of gaol fever that infected the chamber of justice.

At last they had reached the end of the hall and Sir

Percy stopped to gaze at a vast painting of a wheel on the wall above their heads. "Observe the Wheel of Fortune, Fustian," he proclaimed. "It is a symbol of life – the ever turning wheel." He puffed out his chest. "For some of us will rise to fame and fortune," he said majestically, fixing Fustian with a pitying eye, "and *others* will sink into obscurity and decay."

He whirled theatrically through the great oak doors of Westminster Hall and out into the afternoon sunshine on the banks of the River Thames. Fustian followed at a safe distance. "Now hurry along, you dawdling dabchick," he cried. "You and I have some planning to do." He tapped his nose confidentially. "Tomorrow we are to leave with the Chief Justice for the assizes, but I have a cunning trick up my sleeve. I can't have Sir Henry de Mandeville interfering like last time and saving the filthy wretches from the gallows." He laughed cruelly, baring his horsy teeth. "So I mean to get away without him, Fustian – give our Chief Justice the slip!"

Fustian's shoulders drooped almost to the ground. "God help the poor rabble," he mumbled.

"What did you say, you scrawny sparrow?"

"I said, I'll prepare the saddles, Sir Percy," replied the melancholy clerk, pulling a lock of his stringy hair.

Sir Percy shot Fustian a withering glance. His clerk was rather frayed to say the least, but then what could you expect for a penny a day? "Now then, you cantankerous old crow," he growled, twisting his silken sash into the shape of a noose, "are you coming to watch the sport by the horse pond, or not?" He slipped the sash daintily over

Fustian's scraggy neck and pretended to pull. "I can't think of a better way to spend my last afternoon in London."

Chapter 16

A Good Little Knitter

Tom and Herbert wormed back down the warming room flue and wiped their sooty hands on their robes.

"Heavens, where did you two spring from?" yelped Odo as he staggered past the door, carrying a basket full of bell clangers.

"Oh, just … er … turning the cheeses …" said Tom.

Odo looked suspicious. "Well if you've nothing better to do, you can help us fix these clangers back in the bells," he said, his mouth like a prune. "Prior Solomon's making changes already. Bells will be pealing all day and night and everyone will be getting up for Matins – even you!"

"We can't," lied Tom quickly. "Brother Dunstan's given us our own job. Edge trimming in the graveyard." He slipped into the infirmary passage pulling Herbert behind him.

"I didn't know about the graveyard," grumbled Herbert,

shaking Tom's hand from his robe. "I thought we were going to the beast house. I'm getting indigestion with all this racing around."

"Shh! Keep your voice down," whispered Tom. "Don't be silly, Herbert! I made that up about the edge trimming. I mean to visit Mistress Pug in her cottage right now. Find out what old Job really was doing on the night of the murder. The beast house will have to wait. Ethelwig was lying and we need to find out why. You heard Bessie. We've no time to lose. The assizes could be any day now!"

A hideous squawking issued from the pharmacy as they tip-toed down the infirmary passage. Through the half open door they could hear Brother Silas's querulous voice. An untidy note was pinned to the planks:

Caladrius in training.
Do not disturb!

They crept past quickly and out into the shimmering afternoon, skirted the infirmary garden and scrambled over the mossy wall of the monks' burial ground – a short cut to the abbey gate. "We can hardly ask Ethelwig directly," explained Tom, as he tumbled down on top of Herbert into the feathery grass. "He'll just tell the same lie if he's covering up for old Job. So we'll have to ask Mistress Pug instead."

A mound of moist black earth lay steaming in the centre of the graveyard under the crooked yew. The sexton had dug deep for Abbot Theodore, and a pool of muddy water lay in the bottom of the empty hole. Two novices were asleep with their mouths open next to an empty weed bucket but little Edmund was wide awake, sitting cross legged on a tombstone making a daisy chain.

"Where are you two going?" he asked, jumping down.

Tom's heart sank. "Nowhere," he replied evasively. He really didn't want Ed in tow.

"Oh let him come," said Herbert. "We're only going to visit Mistress Pug."

Tom opened his mouth to protest but Herbert already had his arm around Ed's shoulders and was steering him past the open grave.

From the east gate of the abbey it was only a few minutes walk past a straggle of cottages to the edge of the forest where the Pug family lived with their unruly brood of children. As they passed the smithy, the blacksmith waved his hammer at the boys, the powerful muscles on his arms glistening with sweat.

"Hello there, little one," he called cheerily to Ed. "Got any more jobs for me today?" But Edmund hurried on, without even an answering wave.

"What was that about, Ed?" said Tom. "What jobs do *you* have for the blacksmith?"

Ed looked blank. "I think he's confusing me with somebody else," he lisped.

All of a sudden there was a commotion in the bushes. Two barefoot boys tumbled out of the undergrowth into their path in a twitter of giggles, their hands stained black with bilberry juice; exact miniatures of old Job, from their button noses to their short bandy legs.

"Is your mother at home?" asked Tom.

"Course she is. She's minding Baby Amos," said one, with a gappy smile.

"And helping the Virgin Mary with her knitting!" smirked the other.

Job Pug's cottage nestled in a ferny clearing underneath a broad arch of oak branches that formed a tangled canopy, dappling the thatch with patches of light and shade. Mistress Pug sat outside the low door, rocking a wooden cradle with her foot, a piece of grey knitting quivering on her bone needles as they flashed to and fro. A cross-legged girl sat by her feet, tearing a large piece of blue cloth into squares. She stopped what she was doing and stared at the boys, her rosy lips parted.

Mistress Pug got up with a groan, her hand on her back. Her tired blue eyes were rimmed with red. "She's cutting up Saint Peter's sail cloth to sell to the pilgrims," she said, smiling fondly at the little girl. *The actual sail of the blessed saint's boat!* We've done well with relics this summer. It would have been a good year for the Pugs if it hadn't been for our little 'un ..."

The three boys followed her gaze towards a child's chair on the other side of the doorway, where a small pair of leather sandals had been neatly arranged next to a ball of wool and the first few rows of a piece of knitting.

"He was a good little knitter was my Obadiah," she said, dashing a tear away with her finger. "I always bring his chair out into the sunshine."

Tom fidgeted awkwardly. This wasn't such a good idea after all. Baby Amos began to cry and Mistress Pug bent into the cradle and picked him up in her thin brown arms.

"A year to the day, yesterday," she said, her voice trembling. "And at last that fat monk is dead! If only somebody had done away with 'im before now, God forgive me … our little Obi might still be with us." A tear rolled over her eyelid and splashed onto the baby's fuzzy head. "Still," she said, swallowing hard, "I must keep myself strong for my little ones."

Herbert glanced pointedly at Tom and motioned with his head towards the track. "We'll be getting along then," said Tom quickly. "Er … we were only looking for beech nuts." But Mistress Pug was in full flow.

"I thought my Job would die of grief those first few terrible weeks. He went to that wretched beast house *every* day and just stared through the bars into the lion's cage. I don't know what we'd have done without Brother Ethelwig," she murmured, her lips on the baby's head. "I was that glad when the dear Brother said he'd take Job to *The Frisky Friar* last night. *'Don't you go to that beast house on your own,'* I said to Job. *'It won't do you no good, and it won't bring our precious lamb back neither.'"*

There was a silence. Tom cleared his throat. "So Job was in *The Frisky Friar* with Brother Ethelwig last night?" he said.

"And thank the Good Lord, he was," said Mistress Pug, squeezing the baby so tight that it began squeal like a piglet. "If I hadn't known he was safe with dear Ethelwig, I might have thought my Job had done the bursar in himself!"

"Things are looking black for old Job," said Tom grimly as they trudged despondently back along the path from

Mistress Pug's. "He must have lied to his wife to cover his tracks, unless of course she's lying too, and they've worked out the story together."

"Well I vote we say nothing," said Herbert firmly. "We should never have come in the first place. Brother Benedict was a wicked man and Job Pug had good reason to hate him."

"But you're totally missing the point," sighed Tom. "I felt as bad as you did – intruding on Mistress Pug, but Eli Abrahams is in prison – for a crime he probably didn't commit. I don't want Job Pug to go to the gallows any more than you do, but if we keep quiet about this, an innocent man will be hanged."

Chapter 17

Crossed Fingers

Over at Tirley Grange, Abigail Abrahams had abandoned her post at the gate. She'd grown tired of watching for Bessie to come springing across the stepping stones, and had begun to follow the miller around again like a hungry dog, begging for scraps information.

"I've told you already, my dear," shouted Gabriel Miller, above the noise of tumbling water. He was covered in flour from head to foot, his scarlet face streaked with white smudges and dripping with sweat in the heat of the granary. "I went to the town and I spoke to the constable. There's nothing more we can do until the Justices arrive, and that could be any day now. So why don't you go and help Mistress Miller with the baking, or run to the gate again to see if Bessie's back?"

Abigail wrung her fine boned hands together anxiously. "So Father seemed all right to you, Master Miller?" she asked for at least the fourth time.

"Oh, he's comfortable enough. He has food and water and thank the Lord for summer weather," said the miller uneasily, fighting down a memory of Eli's bruised face as he crouched in chains in the damp cell of the town lockup. "Ah, here's Bessie," he said with relief. This was a bad business and it wasn't going to get any better with the autumn assizes due. Pray God the Chief Justice wouldn't bring that pompous upstart with him this time – the one with a taste for torture.

Bessie ducked under the round-headed doorway into the granary. "Now you mind your fingers in the grindstone, Bessie," said Gabriel, smiling at his daughter. He reached across Abigail's skirt, twisted some thick stalks of corn from a fat sheaf and presented them to Bessie with a playful bow.

"Now take Abigail back to the house and make some corn maidens out of these. You're in my way. Oh, and ask your mother to fetch me a jug of ale."

Bessie sat at the freshly scrubbed table, dividing the stalks of corn into two neat piles. "I'll show you how to twist the stems together," she explained to Abigail. "You can make any shape you like: a bell or just a spiral, but it has to be hollow inside. Father says it makes a home for the corn spirit until we plough him back into the first furrow after harvest."

Alice Miller glanced fondly at her daughter. "Your father's a wise man," she smiled. "He becomes quite poetic at reaping time." She was kneading the dough, one end of a split log between her knees. "He says the harvest is like love. If you tend it, it grows up strong and straight, but if you starve it of care, it withers away." She paused, leaning into the dough, a distant light in her eyes. "But love can always spring again in time – like the wheat. When you're as old as I am, you'll understand."

There was a silence. Bessie looked oddly at her mother. She sometimes wondered whether Alice had a secret – not necessarily a sad one, but a secret all the same.

Alice glanced quickly away, breaking the spell with a light laugh. "I'd better take your father his ale," she said hurriedly, rolling the sticky dough from her fingers. "He can turn from poetic to petulant in no time at all if he feels I'm neglecting him."

Bessie watched her mother as she bent under the lintel, the ale jug in her hand. "So you bind the stalks together like this, Abbi," she said, speaking loudly until she was sure her mother was out of earshot. Then she leant quickly across the table. "Everything's going to be all right, Abbi. Tom's going to help us. He's going to investigate the murder from inside the monastery – look for clues to help us find the real murderer. Then, when the King's Justices arrive, we'll be able to clear your father's name. Now that the Pope has banned trial by ordeal, there'll be a fair examination – in front of all the townspeople."

Abigail looked unconvinced. "Fair for the likes of you maybe, but not for people like us. Jews have no legal rights! We're lower than vermin. So even if Father did have one of these new kinds of trial, it would be no fairer than trial by water or fire …"

"Oh don't look so downcast," said Bessie. "Remember our plan. We'll sneak out and visit Eli tonight and see for ourselves how he is." Bessie paused, winding a stalk of corn round her finger. She hadn't told Abbi the whole plan yet. "And … I thought we might visit Jewry Lane. After all … you could do with some clothes …" said Bessie artfully, "and maybe we could look at your father's ledgers whilst we're there – see if we can discover who really was pawning the monastery treasure. You see, Tom doesn't believe it was Brother Fergus. He thinks there might be a link … between the abbey treasure and the murder."

Abigail looked doubtful. "Father was always very secretive about his clients – he wouldn't like to think of me prying," she said reluctantly. "But … he did show me where he hid his records, so that if ever anything happened to him I'd know where to find them …"

"Good," smiled Bessie. "That's settled then." She froze, sensing someone at her back. Gabriel Miller had taken off his wet boots and was standing behind her in his woollen stockings, dripping with water from the yard well.

"I hope I didn't hear you cooking up a plan to take Abigail into town. You know there's a curfew. It's much too dangerous and there's nothing useful to be gained."

Bessie spun round, her eyes wide with innocence. "Oh no, Father! Abbi is much too sensible for that." She got up from the table and gave Gabriel a swift hug. "Trust me, Father," she said, her fingers tightly crossed behind her back.

Chapter 18

The Twisted Horn

The floorboards creaked loudly. The two girls held their breath, anxious eyes fixed on the miller's bedroom door, their shadows quivering like shapeless giants on the ceiling. But Gabriel's rumbling snores were the only sound under the slumbering roof as they crept downstairs.

Bessie placed a pewter candlestick on the stone shelf in the larder. She crossed her arms over her chest and tugged her nightgown up over her head to reveal her clothes underneath.

"I don't feel happy about this," said Abigail staring around the larder. A hare hung by its heels from a blackened beam next to a bunch of wild thyme. "I don't care what you say – it's still stealing. Father wouldn't want …"

But Bessie was busy with the carving knife, cutting a generous slice from a wheel of a rabbit pie. "Don't fret so, Abbi! It's all in a good cause. Pass me that cheese rind.

Nobody will notice that's gone." She wrapped it in a muslin cloth and dropped it into her bag next to a stone bottle of ale. "Let's go," she whispered.

The iron bolts seemed to be in league with the creaking floorboards and then the farmyard dog began to bark. Abigail shrank against the door frame, her hands to her face. "Your Father forbade us to go. And just look at the moon. It's like daylight out here."

The harvest moon hung in the sparkling sky like a lopsided cheese, the smallest slice pared away, as if by a frugal housewife.

"Don't be scared, Abbi. You know you want to see your father more than anything, and you daren't venture into Saint Agnes in the day time. As soon as we're over the stepping stones we can keep in the shadow of the blackthorn. We don't even need a lantern. The river's a ribbon of light."

A fox barked from the silvery woods and a barn owl soared by on velvet wings as the girls hurried along, following the line of weeping willows as the river tumbled down the valley and under the stone bridge into the town. The curfew bell had long since tolled its warning to all but the stray dogs of the street.

The dungeon crouched in the shadow of Saint Agnes's Church – a sombre warning to worshippers, low and windowless, except for a line of iron grills set in the wall at shoulder height.

It's all been so easy, thought Bessie as she waited for her friend in the shadows. *How silly of Abbi to be such a coward.* She was just congratulating herself on the success of her plan when she heard a growl that froze her blood. She hadn't reckoned on the night watchman and his slavering dog, which made up in yellow fangs for what his master lacked in teeth.

It all happened so fast. One minute Abbi was crouching by the bars of the gaol whispering urgently to her father and the next, the terrified girls were racing through the churchyard with a hound from hell at their heels. *"Run Abbi! Run!"* screamed Bessie as helter-skelter, they pelted through the gravestones, weaving in and out of the moonlight and shadows, scratching their legs and bashing their shins as they fled on down into the town.

"Duck down behind the midden heap!" hissed Bessie, pushing Abigail roughly to the slimy ground at the back of *The Frisky Friar Inn*. Choking for breath, she thumped down next to Abbi in the stinking mess. "Thank heavens for the alewives," she giggled. "I think the watchman had a jug too many! Did you hear his screams when he tripped over his dog into the horse trough?"

Part of her wanted to laugh with relief – though it hadn't been funny at the time. The watchman had threatened to call the constable! Bessie crouched like a hare, ears alert for any sound of a hue and cry, but all was silent as the grave – save for the scuttle of black rats in the dung heap. Bessie pinched her nose against the stench. "I don't suppose you had a chance to ask about the treasure," she breathed, looking at Abbi for the first time since their flight. She frowned. Abigail was crying silently, her thin shoulders heaving. "Poor Father," sniffed Abbi. "I didn't even have time to give him the pie – and he looked so frail and ill …"

Bessie felt suddenly ashamed. She was oddly excited, thrilled by their lucky escape and half enjoying the adventure. She'd been thoughtless. Of course Abbi had more important things on her mind. Bessie squeezed Abbi's shoulder. "Come on," she whispered. "At least we can visit your house as we planned – fetch you some clean clothes."

A child's hoop and a whip-and-top lay forgotten on a friendly doorstep, echoes of the busy day in the moonlit silence of Fleshmonger Street, but Jewry Lane felt different. Most of the once prosperous stone houses lay empty, their horn shutters hanging loose like ragged clothes.

"I'm scared, Bessie," whispered Abigail, her hand on Bessie's arm. "Why don't we just go home?"

But Bessie shook her off, rummaging stubbornly in her gown for a stump of candle. She struck a flint to raise a spark. "Come on, I'll go in first," she breathed, holding the candle high.

As their eyes adjusted to the gloom, Abigail let out a sharp cry. The thugs had done their worst. Every cupboard door hung open, hinges broken, bits of pottery scattered and trampled underfoot. Silently, Abigail picked up her father's fringed prayer shawl and held it to her lips. Bessie gazed around in wonder at the unfamiliar objects, the scrolls of the Torah that poked out from the top of their thick velvet mantle, the Sabbath candlesticks and the Kiddush cup that lay on its side on a table. She picked up a ram's horn, inscribed with strange square writing, and looked questioningly at Abigail as if seeing her friend for the first time.

"It's Hebrew," said Abbi – "the language of the Jews. Our holy book is written in it."

"Can you read it?" whispered Bessie in awe.

Abbi nodded. "Love the Lord your God with all your heart …" she read over Bessie's shoulder.

"But that's the same as in our Bible," breathed Bessie, a shiver running down her spine.

She jumped as Abigail grabbed her arm, her hand to her mouth. "I think there's a light in Father's room!"

Bessie placed her finger on her lips. In a second, she had slipped off her shoes and was tip-toeing barefoot towards the door that led to the passage.

In the moneylender's room, the Menorah was alight, all nine flames burning strong and straight in the unmoving air. "Someone's been in the house," breathed Abigail. Look! The candles have only just been lit. They're hardly burnt at all!"

Bessie felt her stomach drop away. "Whoever it was could still be here!"

"No. I think we disturbed them," Abbi whispered, peering down the narrow corridor to where the back door hung open, creaking gently on its hinges. "Let's get out of here before something worse happens."

But Bessie had other plans. "No Abbi!" Her eyes blazed in the candle flame. Abbi could go if she liked, but Bessie was staying here until she'd found exactly what she'd come for. Someone else had been snooping in this house tonight. *It's not only me that thinks there's something here worth looking for,* thought Bessie. *Who could it be and what did they want?* She stared around at the empty chests. "Listen,

Abbi! You must tell me where your father keeps his records," she pleaded. "If we don't take them – somebody else will."

Abigail bit her lip. She didn't want to betray her father's trust, but then again … "Take the end of this trunk then," she relented, "but let's be quick."

The two girls heaved on the chest. If it hadn't been for the sound of scraping iron, they might have heard the noise of shuffling footsteps. If they hadn't been so preoccupied, they might have sensed that someone was creeping stealthily down the passage outside.

The girls sank back on their heels. A long cedar casket lay in a hole in the earth floor. Abigail wanted to take the box – it seemed more respectful to her father's documents – but Bessie was adamant. "We might have to make a run for it again," she explained, rolling the sheaves of thick parchment into a tube, taking pains to keep the wax seals intact. Abbi watched as Bessie stuffed them into the open mouth of her bag. Neither of them noticed the shadows lurching on the uneven wall.

"Now let's get out of here," said Bessie, spinning round with a shriek of terror at a savage growl from the open doorway. Her heart lurched. She stumbled to her feet, clutching the bag to her thundering chest. The town constable filled the frame. The drunken watchman hovered at his elbow, but it was the sober constable who held the drooling dog on the leash. He spoke softly, but Bessie could hear the hatred trembling in his voice.

"Now you do just as I say or I'll set this dog on you," he warned, edging slowly across the small room, brandishing a pair of manacles. "Your little heathen friend is coming with me tonight." He seized Abigail roughly by the arm, twisting it cruelly behind her back. "And as for you, Bessie Miller," he spat contemptuously, "you'd better scarper if you know what's good for you! Get back to your father! And you can tell him from me that I'll teach him how to use a horse whip!"

Bessie winced but her anger was rising, boiling up inside her, steadying her fear. "I'm not going anywhere," she hissed through gritted teeth. "I'm not scared of you. I'm staying with Abbi. Where she goes, I go!"

The constable gaped in disbelief, his hand twitching on the dog's leash.

"No, Bessie," said Abigail, shaking her head. She sounded strangely calm, almost relieved that the waiting was over. "Run home Bessie, while you still have the chance," she said steadily. "This is nothing to do with you."

Bessie looked wildly from the constable to her friend and back to the snarling dog at his feet. "Get out of here, Jew lover," he snarled, "or I'll set this dog on your friend, as God is my witness!"

Bessie shrank away. "I'm sorry Abbi," she whispered, tears welling in her eyes. The dog growled again, more ferociously than before. She could see the whites of its eyes.

"Please do as he says, Bessie," said Abigail, her gaze fixed on the dog.

With an anguished sob, Bessie turned and fled down Jewry Lane, past *The Frisky Friar* and out into Fish Street, across the moonlit churchyard and out onto the stony bridge that spanned the River Twist. She stopped for breath, her body wracked with sobs. An owl screeched and a mouse squealed its dying breath as the desolate girl stumbled on along the river bank, feet bare and bleeding, a bulging bag in one hand and a twisted ram's horn clutched tightly in the other.

August 3rd 1220

Chapter 19

A Broken Whistle

A horse screams. A dying soldier cries out in pain and the ribs of the ship groan in agony. The ocean bulges into rounded hills and then into mountains, jagged and crested with foam. The wind beats in the ragged rigging and the ship is a stallion, riding the monstrous heights of water as the ocean sweeps over the prow. A small boy crouches alone below deck, his head clutched in his thin brown hands and sobs. He is not weeping from bitter cold or biting hunger, or from terror at the screech of the wind in the canvas or the fury of the wild ocean. He is crying for his mother.

A horny hand grasps his shoulder, a soldier's hand, a hand that has slaughtered many men, and yet its owner's face is gentle and around the warrior's neck hangs a jewelled cross. The boy looks up, tears in his black eyes. The soldier takes the child's hand in his. "I am your father now," says Abbot Theodore.

Prior Solomon awoke with a start at the sound of a bell, his body drenched in sweat, the vivid dream still fresh in his mind. It was dark and rain beat on the horn shutters like a ship's drum. Strange how it always rained for a funeral. The bell clanged again for Prime. Wearily he searched in the rushes for his silken slippers. He must hurry to the church to say mass and then prepare himself for Abbot Theodore's farewell. He passed a weary hand over his troubled brow. There was so much to be done to battle the unruly abbey into shape before the Bishop arrived for the election. He wanted to make a good impression. It was well known that the Bishop's vote was crucial and Prior Solomon could have done without the vexing business of the sacristy treasure, hard on the bloody heels of the murder in the beast house.

The monks and novices had hitched up their robes and a procession of grimy white legs, splashed to the knees with sticky mud, filed after Abbot Theodore's lurching coffin towards the yawning black mouth of the grave. Tom felt empty inside as the great abbey bell began its funeral tolling. Sometimes he found it stirring – hauntingly beautiful like the heartbeat of the abbey. But at others he hated its stifling sound and he longed to escape, away to the wild green sea.

Prior Solomon's face was a mask as he intoned a sombre prayer as the coffin was lowered into the mud. Tom scanned the solemn faces of the monks, meeting Brother Dunstan's hateful gaze without flinching and coming to rest on Ethelwig's bony nose – skewed to one side. The old monk looked suddenly sinister. *Why had he lied about Job Pug?* Tom had climbed the tower after Vespers last night to talk to him but Ethelwig had slammed the door in his face. He'd heard Job's voice too and yet Ethelwig had sworn he was alone! *Nothing makes sense,* thought Tom. *The arrest of the moneylender is too convenient. And it's just too neat – for the sacristy treasure to turn up in his house on the night of Brother Benedict's death!* Tom chewed his lip impatiently. *Will this funeral never be over?* He bounced up and down on the balls of his feet. He was desperate to get off to the beast house. He'd volunteered to feed Delilah – an excellent excuse for a snoop.

Brother Silas stalked forward, a clod of black earth in his hand. It dropped heavily onto the coffin lid with a moist thud. And at last the senior monks filed off. Tom sighed with relief. Maybe he could take a look in the bursar's counting house at the same time as feeding the animals. It was just beyond the lion's cage.

As the boys were making their way to the beast house, Bessie Miller sat huddled on her bed at Tirley Grange, her face red and puffy with crying. Gabriel Miller didn't need the town constable to teach him how to deal with a disobedient daughter.

The gusting wind of the early morning downpour had caught a jug of roses and strewn them over the floor of Bessie's garret room. She had left the wattle shutters wide open when she'd sneaked out of the house with Abbi – no hint then of a rainstorm – and now the sun cast pink fingers of light across the damp rush floor.

Alice Miller knocked on the door, nudging it open with her shoulder. She placed a cup of water and a small loaf on the floor in a pool of rosy light. Bessie turned away. The quiet sorrow of her mother pained her more than Gabriel's white hot anger.

Alice Miller knelt down and began to gather up the broken stems of roses. "We trusted you, Bessie, and you lied to us. Oh you may well weep and say you're sorry," she said, sitting back on her heels, "but you'll never turn back time. You have been thoughtless and selfish and now someone else is paying the price. Who knows what will happen to Abigail?"

"But surely Father can … I mean surely he …" choked Bessie, the tears beginning to ooze once more down her flushed cheeks.

"Your father has done all he can, Bessie," said Alice, getting up from the floor and wiping her hands on her apron. "He has already risked his good name on Abbi's behalf. You know how the townspeople feel about the Jews and we have a business to run. There are other millers who would be happy to take our work – and then what would you do for silver pins?" She glanced reproachfully at Bessie's nightgown, still decorated with the foolishness of the Lammas Day fair. "You will stay in your room until your father says you may leave," she said firmly, closing her chamber door.

Bessie stared miserably at the rough planks. After a moment, she got up from the bed, crossed to the open window and swung herself onto the broad sill, wincing from the effects of Gabriel's birch switch on her bottom.

She wiped her nose on her sleeve and looked out. Her mother was crossing the yard carrying a leather pail. All of a sudden she felt angry. It was so unfair! Her mother must know how guilty she felt. She sniffed in righteous indignation. *Come on, Bessie! You can fight back!* She narrowed her eyes so that only a glint of black could be seen. When she opened them again a new Bessie stared out. After all, she had only been trying to help. She squared her shoulders. "And I still have the documents safe in the bag," she told herself, with a calculating smile.

A horse whinnied below her window. Gabriel Miller stood in the yard dressed for the town, his foot in the stirrup. He took the reins from Alice and spoke in her ear, squinting up at his daughter's casement above. Bessie shrank back into the shadows as she heard the clip clop of the horse's hooves over the baked earth yard. She stole another furtive glance. Her mother was walking towards the granary.

Bessie scampered over to her bed and dragged her bag from under the mattress. Her fingers fumbled as she pulled out the thick roll of parchment and began to leaf through the documents, examining each in turn.

"Wedding bands and a blacksmith's hammer," she muttered, twisting a black curl around her finger. "Nothing to do with the abbey. Aha! This is more like it ... one jewelled chalice ..." She smiled as she ran her finger over the seal at the bottom of the bond. Now here was some news for Tom!

Tom and Herbert talked little as they cautiously skirted Delilah's cage. Tom tried not to look at the lioness but his eyes seemed to swivel with a will of their own. Delilah was squatting on the hard earth, her huge shoulders hunched. The gruesome pile of straw had gone but a dirty mark remained. Herbert made a face. "Surely we don't really have to feed her?"

"Someone already has," shuddered Tom. "She's chewing a bone!"

As he turned in disgust from the lion's cage, his foot crunched on something hard that cracked beneath his leather sandal. He bent down to scrabble in the dirt. "Hey, Herbert! Take a look at this. Now where have you seen this before?"

Herbert caught his breath. There in the palm of Tom's outstretched hand lay the crushed remains of a child's whistle on a frayed leather thong.

"Clue number one," said Tom. "This mystery might be easier to solve than we thought."

But the beast house revealed no further clues. "We might as well look in the counting house whilst we're here," said Tom. "If anyone comes we'll tell them we're feeding the lion."

Brother Benedict's office was once the abbey dovecote. It stood behind the beast house, a circular thatched building, surrounded by dense clumps of vicious nettles – the ones with the painful sting that penetrate the thickest cloth. Brother Benedict had added an iron knocker in the shape of a lion's head to the sturdy oak entrance. As Tom had expected, the door was locked.

"Just think," whispered Herbert. "Brother Benedict will never come here again. He's dead."

Tom gave a forced laugh. "Stop it, Herbert! You're making me nervous. Look – there's a window high up," he said, determined to be practical. "Let's see if we can scramble up using the flight holes."

Tom climbed up like a monkey but Herbert found it harder, even with the flight holes for his feet and then he got stuck in the window. It would have been funny if they hadn't felt so tense.

The round room smelt damp from lack of air, the only daylight entering through the pigeon holes in criss-crossed shafts of dusty light. Tom stared in dismay at the mess of tumbled papers on the floor. "Somebody's beaten us to it!" he frowned.

The great seal of the abbey lay on the ground next to a shattered block of sealing wax. Lists and bills had been torn down from nails on the walls and a chest gaped open opposite a disordered table, its lock broken. "Shh!" warned Tom with a sudden start.

"What?"

"Shhhhh!" Tom's eyes were on the door. "There it is again. Can't you hear it?" He put his finger to his lips. The latch sprang upwards and fell back down with a clatter.

The boys held their breath. Neither of them moved but the iron latch lay still. A few long seconds passed. And then a soft scrunching sound broke the silence, followed by the gentle rasp of robes, swishing through the damp grass outside, moving away from the counting house.

Tom's shoulders relaxed. "Probably just a coincidence," he muttered, tip-toeing across the untidy floor and squinting through one of the flight holes. "It could have been anyone

– just passing by. Now let's get on with this and head out of here."

There were a number of letters amongst the mess of parchment on the floor. "Look!" hissed Tom, grabbing one from the heap. "This one's from Brother Benedict to Gabriel Miller – about the lease on Tirley Grange."

If you do not agree to my proposals for a rent increase on your water mill, I will build a new wind mill on Barrow Hill.

Tom sneaked the parchment quickly into the folds of his robe along with the broken remains of the bone whistle. This was a letter he'd definitely not be showing to Bessie. "You're very quiet Herbert," he said. "Hey, what are you doing?"

Herbert was rummaging around in the bursar's desk, his eyes closed in concentration. "Something's moving at the back here," he said in a strained voice. "There's a kind of knob. You try Tom – my fingers are too fat."

Tom knelt down and reached both arms deep into the drawer. "Ouch!" he yelped with a grimace of pain that turned just as suddenly into a gasp of surprise. "Hey, Herbert! Guess what?" He pulled a bundle of parchment from the back of the drawer. "There's a false back to this desk," said Tom excitedly. "And just look at these. They look like letters."

Chapter 20

Sweeter Than Honey

"Love letters!" squealed Herbert, hugging himself in delight. "Come on, Tom. Keep reading."

"Your love is sweeter than honey and the honeycomb ... and next to it the lustre of gold is worthless ..." Tom rolled back against the parapet of the Swallows' Nest, kicking his legs in the air. "I can't believe it! Brother Benedict had a lover! Listen to this end bit," sighed Tom, his hand on his heart. *I am like a hungry little bird. I sigh for you at every hour! Farewell, your Turtle Dove.'"*

Herbert groaned in frustration. "Isn't there a signature? Aren't we going to find out who the lucky lady is?"

Tom grinned. "I bet she looks like a sow and smells like a latrine!" He began to gather up the scattered letters, stacking them into a neat pile.

"I don't suppose we should be prying really," said Herbert half-heartedly.

"Who cares about that?" scoffed Tom, winding a saffron ribbon back around the bundle. "Brother Benedict's dead. Anyway, we're wasting precious time. Love letters won't help us solve this mystery. There are far more important things we need to find out. Such as what Job Pug was doing at the lion's cage. This definitely looks like Obadiah's whistle – the one Job wears round his neck!"

"And who made such a mess in the counting house?" said Herbert. "What were they looking for? I shouldn't think it was love letters."

Suddenly the ivy shuddered on the parapet. "Bessie!" exclaimed Tom, alarmed at the look on her face.

"Thank God I've found you here! You'll never believe what's happened now?" she blurted. "Abbi's been arrested too!"

Tom chewed the side of his nail impatiently, his frown deepening at the news that someone had been in Eli's house before the girls, and turned it upside down. "Maybe it's the same 'someone' who had ransacked Brother Benedict's office before we got there," he said.

"Well I feel terrible about it all," groaned Bessie. "It's entirely my fault. Abbi didn't want to go to the town in the first place but I made her, and now look what's happened! We did find something though – just before the constable turned up with his dog." She held out the sealed bonds she'd taken from Eli's house. "Abbi knew her father's secret place."

Tom snatched the roll of parchment eagerly and began to scan the pages. "It's all there," said Bessie. "All the monastery treasure accounted for. Look! There's a seal at the bottom. If we can discover the owner of the seal, then Brother Fergus will be in the clear about the sacristy treasure. That's something at least, although it doesn't help poor Abbi."

The seal was large, about the size of a squashed conker. Tom ran his thumb over the wax impression of Saint Wilfred, holding a ship in his right hand. He shook his head sadly. "It doesn't add anything, I'm afraid. It's just the plain abbey seal belonging to Abbot Theodore – and it couldn't possibly have been him." He leafed gloomily through the sheets of parchment. "It's clear this has been going on for months. The dates prove it. But Abbot Theodore was away from Saint Wilfred's for so much of this time. And look at this last sheet – it's dated Lammas Day – a bond for two embroidered altar cloths – but the abbot was already dead on Lammas Day – unless his ghost was using the seal!"

Bessie looked crestfallen. "There is something else on the parchment," she said uncertainly. "There were lots of records of pawned items – wedding bands, that sort of thing – and in every case there was a signature or a cross. But look at these abbey bonds. She traced her finger over a pattern of blocky letters at the bottom of a page. "It's Hebrew," she said softly. "And there's the same pattern of letters on *every* document that relates to the abbey treasure. If only we could read it. It's probably someone's name."

Tom had never seen Hebrew before. He frowned at the unfamiliar letters as if by staring hard enough they might reveal their secret. *What if someone other than Fergus had a key to the sacristy? Perhaps they'd been using the abbey seal to cover their tracks.* It was clear he'd have to speak to Fergus in the lock-up. But that was going to be easier said than done.

The abbey bell clanged, summoning them to the refectory. "Oh no!" groaned Tom. "We've got Manuscript Illumination with Brother Dunstan after dinner. This new regime is killing me. Bells and timetables, polishing and weeding – things have changed so much, and Abbot Theodore's only been dead two days! Come on Herbert. We'd better get going."

"Wait a minute!" said Bessie sharply. "We need to make a plan. It's more urgent than ever to clear Eli's name now they've arrested Abbi as well. You must question Ethelwig. Trip him up on the lie he told about Job Pug. And see if you can find out what Job was doing at the beast house, now you've found the whistle." She began to stuff the rolls of parchment hurriedly into her bag. "I must go too. I'm not meant to have left my room at Tirley Grange – and I'm certainly not supposed to be here."

"Just one more thing," said Tom, remembering their discovery with a grin. "Take a peep at these before you go. We found them in a secret drawer in Brother Benedict's desk. They don't help us with our investigations but it might cheer you up a bit. They're love letters!"

Bessie glanced at the first sheet without interest. *'My Lord,* she read. *'You alone are my love and my desire ...'* She stopped abruptly, a scarlet flush racing up her neck to her cheeks, and then she turned pale; as white as the feathers on a Caladrius.

"Oh my God," she gasped, her hand to her mouth. She

gazed at Tom, her eyes wide with horror. "Are these all of them?" she asked in a strangled voice.

"Why – what's the matter?"

But Bessie had ears for no one. She caught her breath with a choking sob, and then she was gone, slipping over the parapet and down the twisting ivy, the bundle of letters clutched tightly in her hand.

Chapter 21

A Rancid Eel

Percy FitzNigel, the King's Justice, pulled a pocket sundial impatiently from a well stuffed saddle-bag and held it up to the sky.

"Hurry up, Fustian, you scrawny scragamuffin!" he brayed to his threadbare clerk. He slapped the muscular flank of his chestnut mare. "I don't pay you a penny a day for nothing!"

Fustian muttered something under his breath as he tightened the leather straps around Percy's goose-feather mattress, securing it firmly to the rump of his own broken down old nag.

"What did you say, you rusty raven?" rapped Percy sharply, swinging elegantly into his saddle and adjusting its ermine cover.

"I said a penny a day is more than generous, Sir Percy," cringed the cross-eyed Fustian, pulling his long moustache deferentially. He scrambled onto the saggy back of his ancient packhorse and was soon lost amidst the piles of silken cushions and sacks of robes essential to the comfort of his master.

Sir Percy nodded approvingly. "I like a man who knows when he's well off, Fustian. You've done yourself proud. A man of your scant learning – clerk to a King's Justice! Now, if you've checked the papers and loaded the boxes we can make start. We've a good few hours riding before sunset. We'll be in Saint Agnes Next-the-Sea before Sir Henry can safely leave the latrine!"

Grinning in complacent delight, he trotted off, the iron hooves of his mount sparking on the cobbles. And who could blame an ambitious young lawyer, who had studied law in Oxford and Paris, for slipping a rancid eel onto the trencher of Sir Henry de Mandeville, his fellow justice, and senior by more than thirty years?

"Such a shame that Sir Henry finds himself confined to his closet," hooted Percy merrily as they rode out of London into the golden afternoon. "It seems I will have to attend the county assizes all by myself. I will then put in a report to the King that I have done the work of two Justices in half the time!"

They were fording a small stream, Fustian's short legged pony up to her belly in the water, his own holey boots well beneath the surface. Percy splashed through easily on his long legged mare.

"You're an ambitious man, Sir Percy," muttered Fustian gloomily.

"Hurry up, you old starling," laughed Percy, twisting in his saddle. "Keeping in with the King and the Archbishop is everything, and if this mission helps me to become Chief Justice, I'll raise your wages to tuppence a day!"

Sun scorched peasants dragged off their caps as Sir Percy rode through fields where men in smocks laboured in a line, scything the summer crop. A straggle of grey-legged partridges followed the reapers, pecking at the leavings. Sir Percy chewed happily on a juicy apple. "I only hope there'll be something a little more interesting for us in Saint Agnes this year. We didn't send a single soul to the gibbet or cut off anybody's ears at the last assizes. I wouldn't mind so much if it wasn't for that spineless Pope outlawing Trial by Ordeal. These new fangled jury trials are no sport at all. I'll never understand why King John Softsword agreed to them, God rest his black heart."

"I thought the idea was that the new trials would be a bit f...f ... fairer," stammered Fustian, cringing behind a pile of silk cushions almost before the words had escaped from his mouth.

Percy FitzNigel spun indignantly in his saddle. "Who gave you permission to burble, Fustian? What's wrong with a little trial by scalding? Mmm," he groaned luxuriously, as if tasting a luscious sweetmeat, "the excitement of peeling off those bandages to see if God has healed the tender flesh – it used to bring tears to my eyes – tears of joy, that is!" He sighed regretfully. "If there's nothing better for us to sink our teeth into than a bit of wife beating, then let's hope Sir Ranulf de Lacy can lay on a decent boar hunt."

But Fustian was out of earshot; his old pony staggering under the weight of Sir Percy's bulging bags and iron bound boxes.

"Get off and walk for a bit, you crumbling crow," called Percy heartlessly. "Can't you see you're too heavy for poor Griselda? What do you mean my mattress isn't necessary? Last time we stayed with Sir Ranulf de Lacy, he only lent me his second best straw!"

Chapter 22

Emerald Silk

Bessie crept stealthily around the corner of the tithe barn at Tirley Grange, her breath short from running. The mill was busy and sharp shouts of workers rose above the slow laboured grind of the millstones and the lazy swoosh and tumble of the waterwheel. But the yard was empty. She scampered across, skirted the square stone house, and slipped in by the larder door at the back. Bessie could hear her mother in the kitchen – the steady rocking sound of the kneading log on the hard earth floor. Fixing her eyes on the door, she trod softly backwards up the stairs, the bundle of letters clutched in her hand. She pressed the latch of her parents' bedchamber gently, cringing at the sharp click.

The room smelled of the lavender and tansy her mother used to sweeten the bed and keep the fleas at bay. Alice's clothes chest stood under the window, a stray piece of russet fabric trapped in the lid. Bessie's black eyes flicked guiltily over her father's rough shirt that lay on the bed, his working boots askew on the floor beside a wicker basket full of mending. It was a bare space, rough and workaday, except for a forlorn lute, propped in the corner, gathering dust. Bessie stared hard at the wooden chest. It was the only place in the simple room where a secret might be concealed.

Bessie pressed her hand to her throat and swallowed, as if pressure would calm the uneven rhythm of her heart. The mellow rocking sound of Alice kneading the dough still came from the kitchen. With an anxious glance at the door, Bessie crept like a thief towards the iron bound trunk and, trembling, lifted the lid.

The linen was rough; madder brown and bone yellow – the colours of earth and hedgerow – aprons and shifts and plain woollen tunics, neatly folded, sweet herbs in between. Bessie pressed aside the layers, releasing the lemony smell of tansy, groping down with her fingers to the silken fabric beneath the coarser weaves. She pulled. Out slid a sky blue bodice laced at the back with golden silk to reveal the glimpse of a crimson tunic underneath. It whispered as she tugged it free and delved once again into the forbidden chest. A knotted belt of tassels and beads snaked into the sun entangled in a necklace of sea green stones. Bessie scrambled to her feet and tip-toed to the door. Her mother was singing in the kitchen: *'Farewell my joy, and welcome pain, until I see my Lady again ...'*

Bessie turned back to the trunk and heaved the clothing onto the rush floor, plain wool and un-dyed linen making way for satins and silks, velvets and brocades, until her fingers scraped on the uneven base of the chest. There in the bottom, hiding in a corner underneath a muslin veil, lay a bundle of letters. As she snatched them up, a splinter of wood slid painfully between her nail and the soft cuticle beneath. Biting her lip against the smarting throb, she began to stuff the garments hastily back into the chest. She knew she should try to fold the clothes, but how could she explain her presence in her mother's room if she were caught? With a quick look over her shoulder, she laid the topmost woollens neatly back, spattering the final apron with her blood.

'I know of a beauty, a jewel most bright, she's lovely to look on, she gleams in the light ...' sang Alice as she baked in the kitchen.

Bessie glanced around the chamber to check that all was as she'd found it, and then sneaked along the landing to her own room, pulling the door softly behind her.

She sank down on the bed, her fingers shaking as she slipped the saffron ribbon from the first bundle of letters Tom had shown her in the Swallows' Nest. The writing was angular, almost spiky, with just a hint of a forward tilt. It was her mother's script – she would swear on her life!

She unwound the binding from the second bundle of letters – the ones from her mother's chest. This writing was neat and rounded, with long slanting strokes ascending and descending across the parchment. *'My Little Bird,'* read Bessie, tears welling in her eyes, *'You are my love and my desire; you are the sweet refreshment of my soul ...'* She opened each note in turn, scanning to the bottom for a signature – but the writer was playing hide and seek with her behind the curling ink.

Her father, Gabriel, could only write a little, his name and a few other characters – after all, what need had a miller for a quill pen? Alice kept the accounts for him such as they were, for she had been raised as a lady, before she laid her lute in the corner and learnt to bake the harvest bread. A tear splashed onto the parchment in Bessie's trembling hand and the brown ink snaked into life within the pearl of water. One thing was clear – whoever the writing belonged to, it was certainly not her father's. But what mischief had Brother Benedict been up to with a packet of love letters in her mother's handwriting, and who could be replying to Alice with such fiery passion?

Bessie hesitated in the kitchen doorway, breathing in the yeasty smell of freshly baked bread. A neat pyramid of soft white rolls steamed on the table next to her mother's embroidery chest with its dainty inlay of mother of pearl and polished wood. A piece of fine linen lay next to a rectangle of creamy parchment and a bag of powdered charcoal dust. Bessie ran her fingers over the bumpy parchment where her mother had pricked holes in a design of curling flowers and leaves. Later, Alice would lay the design on top of the fabric and press the charcoal bag gently down, so that the soft dust would fall through the holes onto the linen beneath.

"Bessie!" said Alice sharply, bustling in from the yard with a basket of eggs in her arms. Bessie jumped – her nerves like spun sugar. "I thought your father told you to stay in your room until he came home."

"I've been on my own for hours, mother," she said, cringing inwardly at the untruth. "I was wondering if there was any news of Abigail or Eli. Can't I just sit with you until we hear Father's horse?" she begged. "He might bring some news of the King's Justices. And I could help you lay the pattern on the linen whilst we wait for him. You always say it's hard to do it on your own. And besides," she pouted. "My head aches from crying."

Alice's stern look softened. "You do look very flushed," she said, smoothing her daughter's dark hair from her forehead with a cool hand. She pulled Bessie towards her with a sigh, brushing her curls with her lips. "You're too wilful, Bessie Miller," she said softly. "It will only bring you grief. Now let me see if I can find some feverfew in the larder – it will cool your brow. But when you hear your father's horse, you must whirl upstairs like the wind."

Bessie sipped the steaming bitter herbs with a grimace as her mother sat down again to her embroidery.

"What shade of green shall I use for the leaves?" asked Alice. "There's emerald, jade, dusky olive. Your father bought me these colours from a merchant in the town – all the way from heaven alone knows where. He spoils me," she laughed.

Bessie handed Alice a skein of emerald silk, a puzzled look in her eyes. "Mother?"

"Hmmm?" said Alice, squinting as she passed the thread through the needle's eye.

"Why did you choose to marry a miller … you know … when you might have been a lady? You could have lived at

Micklow Manor with cooks and servants and fine clothes and … and spent your days playing the lute instead of baking bread and feeding chickens."

"Bessie!" exclaimed Alice in a shocked tone. She winced as she pricked her finger with the newly sharpened needle.

Bessie's felt her face grow hot. "I … I don't mean that I'm sorry you married Father or anything like that … it's just that … if I'd been born a lady … I don't think I would have …" Bessie's black eyes grew round with the spark of a new idea. "Mother! You don't think Sir Ranulf de Lacy would help clear Eli's name do you? Maybe you could speak to him … ask him to have a word in the Chief Justice's ear."

Alice sucked her finger with more force than necessary. "You know that wouldn't be possible, Bessie," she said sternly. "Oh bother! There's blood on the linen now."

An awkward silence fell between them. Bessie could hear the chickens scratching in the earth outside the door. She thought of the letters concealed beneath the mattress in her room upstairs: *'You are the sweet refreshment of my soul …'* and her mother singing in the kitchen: *'Farewell love and welcome pain.'*

Alice Miller laid the fabric aside with a sigh and gazed at her daughter thoughtfully. Bessie held her mother's eyes as steadily as she could. "Bessie …" said Alice gently. Bessie wanted to swallow, but her throat was dry. "There's something …" Alice paused, her ear turned slightly towards the open doorway, listening. A rhythmic clopping of a horse's hooves echoed across the yard of Tirley Grange.

"Yes, Mother?" said Bessie breathlessly.

"I think your father's home," she laughed a little too loudly, springing up and running to the door. "Better slip upstairs, Bessie," she whispered. "I'll see if I can talk him round. He'll allow you down for supper later on, I promise. I'm roasting a partridge tonight."

Chapter 23

The Pious Pilgrim

As Bessie Miller sat in the kitchen at Tirley Grange, Tom was chewing his squirrel-hair brush in frustration. Manuscript illumination! What a waste of his time – painting flowers onto sheets of parchment when he had so much to do! He was desperate to ask Brother Fergus about the sacristy key. *Did Fergus really have the only one?* Tom had thought of a way of avoiding the eagle-eyed gaoler – but it was going to be risky. He gazed uneasily through the arched window. He'd still not had a chance to speak to Ethelwig about Job Pug and now he had another thing to worry about: Bessie and those wretched love letters! *What had upset her so much?* Brother Dunstan stalked threateningly between the rows of sloping desks, his cane hand quivering. Tom wiggled his knees anxiously, watching the novice master out of the corner of his eye. Time was running out and the mystery was deepening, growing more confused with every passing hour.

"Brother Dunstan," called Odo, in a grovelling voice. "I can't decide between dragon's blood and vermilion for my poppies."

Tom glanced furtively around the illumination room, weighing up the various options for escape. It was going to be hard to slip out unnoticed with Felix on one side and the wall on the other. Slowly, slowly, he edged back his stool. Brother Dunstan was stooping over Odo, his back towards Tom. He turned sharply at the scrape of wood on stone, his eyes bulging, but Tom was firmly in his seat, head bent, intently stirring a brown mess on his page. *This is hopeless! Brother Dunstan has eyes in the back of his robes. And even if I do manage to escape he's bound to miss me. There must be some other way.* With a cautious glance at the bent heads of the other novices, Tom picked up his jay feather quill and began to bend the shaft roughly backwards and forwards, his tongue between his teeth. Then with a sudden cry of surprise, he sprang to his feet.

"Oh Brother Dunstan," he cried. "How clumsy of me! My quill has just snapped! Can I run over to the quillery and ask Brother Ambrose for another one?"

Brother Dunstan wheeled round, his sallow face deepening to a shade of purple as his eyes fell on the muddy mess on Tom's parchment. He took a step towards him, his birch switch quivering. Tom swallowed hard. The novice master was within an arm's length of his desk. There was a sudden rush of air followed by a sickening crack. Tom snatched his hand away with a cry of pain.

"Stings, doesn't it?" said Brother Dunstan with a malicious smile. "Now – you have precisely five minutes to get over to the quillery and collect a new pen," he snarled through gritted teeth. "And if you are not back within that time …"

Tom didn't wait to find out what delights Brother Dunstan had in store. *This had better be worth it,* he thought, clutching his smarting hand as he sped around the cloisters and through the infirmary passage towards the river. He turned suddenly at a noise behind him.

"If you think you're leaving me behind painting flowers, you've another think coming!" puffed Herbert. "I gave old Dunstan the slip as soon as his back was turned!"

Percy FitzNigel clattered under the wide stone arch of *The Pious Pilgrim Inn,* scattering bewildered guests like chickens. He bellowed for the stable boy to water his horse. The sun was sinking behind the timber-framed tavern, gilding the thatch with glowing embers as if at any moment it might kindle into flames. The King's Justice had grown impatient with the heat and had galloped the last mile, leaving Fustian far behind, limping along the dusty track in a halo of buzzing horseflies, leading Griselda – lame with a stone in her shoe. Percy sprang from his horse and hailed a group of travellers who were sipping their ale in the shade of a twisted crab apple tree.

"A splinter of the true cross …" he heard a pilgrim murmur as he concealed a leather purse within the folds of his shirt.

Percy minced up to the group and struck a pose, displaying his bulging calf muscles to their best advantage. "Somebody fetch the landlord this instant!" he boomed.

"Tell him Percy FitzNigel is waiting – and he needs a bed for the night."

The harassed innkeeper scurried into the yard, wiping his hands on a filthy rag. He stared in awe at Sir Percy's silken legs. His own leggings sagged to his ankles as if preparing themselves for an annual moulting.

"I'm … I'm sorry Sir," he stammered, mopping his bald head with the greasy cloth, "but … we don't have an empty mattress." He waved his hand helplessly around the courtyard. "We're full to the rafters with pilgrims you see and … I mean … if I'd only known in advance …"

Percy FitzNigel jerked his neck forward theatrically, twisting his wide mouth with its double row of horsy teeth into a grimace of disbelief. He made a whinnying sound like an impatient mare. The landlord shrank back as if fearful that Sir Percy might bite.

"Then you must raise the rafters for the Chief Justice, you churl," he brayed. "Pluck out a pilgrim. Tease out a traveller. Flush out a friar," he screeched, "or the King himself will hear of it," he added, in a voice as cold as ice.

As Percy FitzNigel was congratulating himself on securing lodgings for himself in *The Pious Pilgrim Inn,* Tom and Herbert were wading through the bulrushes, their robes looped into their leather belts, on their way to the monastery gaol beneath the monks' latrine. The course of the River Twist had been diverted many years ago, so that a small tributary flowed under the wall – an ingenious flushing device. Tom had armed himself with his catapult and a good supply of stones and was now preparing to attract Brother Fergus's attention from the river.

"Whose stupid idea was it to wade through this stinking muck?" grumbled Herbert, slithering in his sandals on the thick sludge of the river bed. "It pongs of rotten eggs! And Brother Dunstan will be livid when he finds me missing and *you've* certainly been longer than five minutes!"

"Stop fussing Herbert and keep in the shadow of the wall," hissed Tom. "I didn't ask you to come and you'll attract attention, floundering around like that. There's no point turning back now. When else will we get a chance to visit Fergus when nobody's about?" His own stomach was heaving. He could feel the greasy mud, oozing between his toes.

It had been easy going at first, splashing through the purple reeds, but now as they were nearing their destination, the stench was intolerable. The clear green river had become a festering stream of yellow brown liquid, punctured with grubby islands of dirty brown foam. Herbert wrinkled his plump nostrils. "I think I'm going to be sick," he gagged.

"Hey, Herbert," whispered Tom. "Do you remember that time when Brother Dunstan sent you up the latrine chute to clear a blockage with a poker? You got stuck in the filthy flue and we all had to pull you out by your ankles!"

Herbert shot Tom a withering glance.

"Sorry," laughed Tom nervously. "I couldn't help remembering. Come on. We'd better hurry before somebody sees us. I'm going to prime the catapult now. I think the gaol's behind that grating in the wall. Let's speak to Fergus and then make ourselves scarce."

The first shot missed the rusty bars entirely, clattering down the stone wall, but the second flew cleanly through, rewarded almost at once by a hairy ginger face at the opening. Brother Fergus's beard was wilder than ever but his face was pale. He peered out over the festering river, his anxious expression lighting up at the sight of the boys.

"Tom! Herbert!" he cried loudly. "By Saint Wilfred's bunion, it's good to see you!"

The boys cringed against the slimy wall. "Shhh!"

"What brings you here? I have nae seen a living soul except the gaoler since yesterday morning, apart from poor Mungo who spends most of his time staring at this wall from the other side of the river."

Tom felt a surge of pity. Brother Fergus looked so forlorn – his big hairy face staring desolately from behind the grill. Tom glanced warily over his shoulder. "Listen!" he said, his hand over his nose against the stink. "We've got to be quick. We don't believe you stole the treasure, but we need to ask you some questions."

Brother Fergus rattled the grill with his fists. "I have to see Prior Solomon," he called back. "He *must* give me a chance to explain about the sacristy key."

"What about it?" hissed Tom. "Tell us quickly! Has it ever gone missing? Have you ever misplaced it?"

"Aye, well," said Fergus, clearing his throat awkwardly, "there was just one occasion when I did lose sight of it – just for a day or two, you understand – a fair few months back now. I remember thinking I must have sent it to the laundress by accident. But she knew nothing of it when I asked her, and then, bless my soul, it turned up in my room! I checked the contents of the sacristy cupboard at the time and there was nothing missing. So I thought nae more about it – I just took a deal more care of the key after that."

"Can you think of anything else that might help us – anything at all?" urged Tom.

"Well there was something strange about the missing key," added Fergus, scratching his beard. "When it turned up – it looked different somehow. And then I noticed it had a film of wax on it. I assumed it was candle grease at the time and I didnae concern myself with it. It's only now I've been thinking ..."

"Tom!" gasped Herbert. "Watch out! Brother Silas – over on the far bank!"

Tom spun round, shrinking back against the latrine wall. He stared in dismay at the figure approaching on the opposite side of the river, stalking through the hairy willow herb like a daddy-long-legs, the Caladrius on his shoulder.

"My God, where did he spring from?" breathed Tom. "And he's got that hideous bird with him!"

"Hey! You two! What are you doing?" Brother Silas's petulant voice rapped angrily from the other side of the narrow river. The Caladrius was on a heavy chain, one end around Silas's wrist and the other around its thick red leg. "You have an uncanny knack of turning up where you have no business to be! Now what are you up to? Trying to talk to Brother Fergus, I'll be bound."

"Oh just p ... pottering about before supper. I ... improving our appetites, you know," stammered Herbert.

"Well there are prettier stretches of river than down by the latrines!" observed the physician tartly. "Now get away from here, the pair of you!"

The sun was low in the sky as the boys waded back through the reeds, past the fat cattle chewing idly in the water meadow and the drowsy hornets in the field thistles.

"What are we going to say to Brother Dunstan?" asked Herbert anxiously. "He'll skin our hides for parchment!"

Tom fingered the blue-black weal on the back of his hand where Brother Dunstan had caught him with the switch. It was really smarting now. "At least it was worth it," he said, flexing his fingers in pain. "It wasn't a wild goose chase this time."

"What do you mean?" asked Herbert. "I'm just as confused as ever."

"But don't you see, Herbert? We've discovered a vital piece of information."

Herbert let a snake of weed slip through his fingers into the water. "If you say so," he frowned.

Tom raised an impatient eyebrow. "Listen, Herbert! Brother Fergus has the only key to the sacristy cupboard, right? One day the key goes missing. A few days later it turns up again covered in wax. Where has it been in the meantime?"

Herbert shrugged. "Your guess is as good as mine."

"No," said Tom firmly. "My guess is a lot better. Think, Herbert. Why would the key be covered in wax? Someone must have made a little trip to the blacksmith's forge with a wax impression of the sacristy key. And I'm going to find out exactly who that somebody was. If we can discover how these events fit together, maybe it will lead us to the murderer!"

The King's Justice sucked on the last remaining blackbird's thigh, savouring the tender meat. His trencher was a mass of pitiful songbird bones, larks and linnets, finches and nightingales. He glanced out of the window, a sneer of satisfaction on his face, as the pilgrims trooped gloomily under the arch in their broad-brimmed hats, their bundles on their backs. He smiled spitefully to himself. The nights could be cold, even in August.

"How's your gruel, Fustian?" he slurped, licking the grease from his lips.

"A bit thin," grumbled the frayed clerk from his dusty corner.

"What's that?" snapped Sir Percy.

"Fit for a King," repeated Fustian mournfully.

There was a knock on the door of the best parlour. It was the saggy landlord, wringing the same filthy cloth in his hands.

"There's a rider arrived from Saint Agnes sir, on his way to London with a message for the Chief Justice. I told him you were here sir – shall I show him in?"

There was a strangled squawk from Fustian's corner.

"Indeed?" said Sir Percy with interest, rinsing his fingers elegantly in a bowl of water and shaking the drops energetically in Fustian's direction. "Tell him that the er … er …" He stared into the corner, glaring Fustian to silence. "…that the *Chief* … Justice will see him directly!"

A crumpled messenger stumbled in, weary from the day's ride but unable to believe his luck. What good fortune to cross paths with the Chief Justice at *The Pious Pilgrim Inn*. He could be back in Saint Agnes by the following afternoon. He pulled off his cap and scraped a low bow to Sir Percy.

"Message from the County Sheriff, my Lord," he said, holding out a folded piece of parchment, sealed with a heavy black disc.

Percy snatched it rudely. He turned the parchment over, his lips moving as he read the direction. "Sir Henry de Mandeville," he smiled, snapping open the seal with a provocative toss of his nose towards Fustian. "Greetings Sir Henry," he read under his breath, his greedy eyes darting along the lines of neat brown writing. Fustian's spoon clunked softly on the earthenware bowl as he chased an elusive pea around the rim. Percy FitzNigel looked up, a buck-toothed smile on his face.

"It seems our luck's changed, you old scarecrow!" he trilled, screwing the letter into a tight ball and aiming it at Fustian's head. "There's been a murder at Saint Wilfred's Abbey! We might have been robbed of our trial by drowning, but at least we'll see somebody twitching on the gibbet before we trot back to London!"

August 4th 1220

Chapter 24

fiery Sparks And
Murky Shadows

*T*he novices' mouths are jeering holes of teeth and tongues, their lips curled back in scorn. Mocking laughter rings in the small boy's ears as the furious monk rips the grey robe over his head and thrusts a bundle of ragged clothes into his skinny arms. His old woollen jacket had only ever fitted by a stretch of the imagination and two years have passed since the day the orphan was found, huddled at the great bronze doors of Saint Wilfred's. The tight sleeves strain around the boy's elbows as he trudges across the outer court of the abbey, tears of shame flowing down his flaming cheeks, past the stables and the brewery, the bake house and the laundry. He is clutching an owl feather quill. The abbey gates are open. The yellow road winds like a discarded ribbon into the empty days ahead. The novice master steps forward, eyes blue as ice. The boy *uncurls his hand and the tawny feather flutters to the ground where a contemptuous sandal grinds it into the grey dust. The small boy screams, covering his face with his hands.*

Ed shot upright on his straw mattress, his own scream in his ears. He pushed a strand of damp blond hair from his forehead. A black trellis of branches danced in the glow of two straight rows of oil lamps, casting a mottled pattern on the two straight rows of sleeping boys in the dormitory.

"What's the matter, Ed?" yawned Tom irritably. "Was it another bad dream?" He gazed, bleary eyed, at the trembling boy in the nearby bed. *What was the matter with Ed these days? He seemed so miserable and yet he used to be always singing.* Tom passed a weary hand over his face. The prior's new regime of services during the night was punishing for everyone.

"Don't cry, Ed," he sighed, scrunching across the rushes towards the small boy's pallet. "Don't think about the dream. Try to think of something nice," he whispered, lowering himself down onto the edge of the straw mattress. "Spiced fig pasties … blackberry picking …" He placed a comforting hand on the trembling blankets. "And conkers … it's nearly conker time," he murmured, his eyes beginning to close.

When the bell rang for the first service of the day, Tom could hardly drag himself from his straw pallet until he suddenly remembered about the wax and the key. Perhaps he could run over to the blacksmith's forge straight after breakfast and ask him about it.

But Brother Dunstan had other plans for him, and

late morning found Tom still scrubbing moss from the tombstones, his stomach a knot of frustration. He squinted impatiently up at the sun, just emerging over the topmost branches of the crooked yew.

Herbert staggered to his feet, beads of sweat on his face. It was backbreaking work. He reached his arms above his head wearily, his robe almost bursting at the seams. "We're luckier than poor Ed," he said, his voice distorted from stretching. "He was skinning eels in the kitchen when I last saw him. He looked shattered."

"I'm not surprised," said Tom tetchily. "His nightmares are wearing *me* out. There's something up with Ed these days but he won't say what it is. Look Herbert – I've got to run over to the blacksmith's for a few minutes to ask about the key."

Herbert looked doubtful. "What's the betting the minute you go, Brother Dunstan will appear to check up on us? He's got eyes everywhere – or spies should I say," he grumbled, thinking of Odo's priggish face.

A clod of earth hit Tom between the shoulder blades, exploding in a spray of grass seeds. He spun round, but the shimmering horizon was empty. And then he saw a mop of black curls bobbing along on the far side of the wall. Bessie at last! Perhaps she'd tell them why she'd dashed off in such a hurry with the letters. Tom glanced quickly around the graveyard to check they were unobserved and then watched anxiously as she hitched up her skirt, tied it into a knot and clambered easily up the lichen crusted wall. Grabbing a tuft of strong grass, she hauled herself over and dropped down into the long grass.

"What was all that nonsense about?" frowned Tom, pulling Bessie behind a tombstone. She stumbled against a bucket of mossy water with a cry.

"Sorry," said Tom. "But we can't let Brother Dunstan see us talking to you. He's got his spies everywhere. So why did you run off with our letters?"

Bessie was strangely agitated, her hands fluttering between her mouth and a soft leather bag around her neck.

"What's the matter? Not more bad news?"

"No news of Abbi, if that's what you mean. It's something else. Look … I'm sorry I rushed off like that yesterday but … I was so shocked!" she gabbled breathlessly, pulling at a wayward strand of hair. "I just couldn't believe my eyes when I saw the letters. I was praying I was wrong all the time … but I had to get home to find out!" She looked desperately at Tom. "Sorry. It's all coming out back to front. You must wonder what I'm talking about."

"Er … just a tiny bit, Bessie," said Herbert, flicking a piece of moss from the top of a headstone.

"Go on, Bessie," coaxed Tom. "We're listening. Try telling it the right way round."

Bessie glanced nervously about the graveyard. "I've got something to tell you about those love letters," she said in a hesitant voice. "I… I recognised the handwriting …" She fumbled in the bag around her neck. "I had a hunch … and I was right. I found these!"

Tom shot her a puzzled glance. "More letters?"

"They're the replies to the ones you found in Brother Benedict's office. You see, the handwriting in those letters … it's my mother's!"

Herbert's eyes widened. "Your mother's?" he gasped. "You mean ... your mother ... and ... and Brother Benedict?"

A tear splashed onto Bessie's hand. "And before you ask, Tom," said Bessie, ignoring Herbert, "the letters definitely go together. They call each other by the same pet names."

Tom shook his head slightly as he took the letters from Bessie's outstretched hand. He opened the first one, his eyes skimming the flowing script. "I see what you mean," he said. He paused awkwardly. "I know what it looks like Bessie, but maybe you're jumping to conclusions. I admit we all had a laugh about the bursar's lady friend but ... that was before we knew about this handwriting. I mean – your mother and Brother Benedict! It's ridiculous!"

Bessie wiped her nose on the back of her hand and sniffed. "I have thought of that, Tom," she said with a watery smile. "I know they're not necessarily *from* Brother Benedict. I don't know how he came to have them, but they are from somebody. Mother's got a lover – and it's not my father. And that fat bursar knew all about it!"

Tom shrugged. "Well he's dead now. He can't spread any rumours from the grave."

Bessie looked up at Tom. "I know that," she said, tears welling again in her eyes, "but it's hardly the point."

The old forge crouched like a beast in the clearing, with roaring bellows for lungs and fire and smoke for breath. Tom had slipped off leaving Herbert still scrubbing away and keeping a sharp look out for the novice master. He felt bad leaving Bessie looking so upset but he had to grab this chance to see the blacksmith. It would only take a minute to ask one simple question. He prayed Brother Dunstan would stay away from the graveyard until he got back.

The blacksmith's brazier throbbed like an angry wound, sending up showers of sparks, as Tom ducked under the oak lintel into the murky shadows, his eyes smarting. An assortment of ironwork lay strewn on wooden trestles: horseshoes, armour, chisels and chains – even a huge anchor was propped against the grimy wall.

"Hello!" called Tom into the fiery darkness. "Anybody home?"

A sooty face emerged from behind the blazing furnace followed by the blacksmith's muscular arms and chest. He was naked to the waist, his leather apron slung low beneath his belly.

"Hello again," he said cheerily. "I don't see a novice for weeks and now you're like acorns in autumn. Come on outside for a drink," he puffed, rearranging the soot on his dripping face with the back of his hand. "It's like the Devil's parlour in here today!"

Tom bit his thumb impatiently whilst the blacksmith ducked his head and shoulders into the water trough outside, emerging in a vigorous spray of dirty droplets. "That's better," he gasped, grinning lopsidedly at Tom. "Now what can I do for you this time?"

"This time?" said Tom with a puzzled smile.

The blacksmith cocked his head quizzically. "No, wait a minute. I'm muddling you up with that little 'un aren't I? Lovely little chap – what's his name? Edward ... Edgar ... *Edmund* – that's it. The one I made the key for."

Tom's stomach dropped like a stone. "E ...Edmund?" he stammered in a horrified voice. "You made a key for *Edmund*?"

"Oooh a good few months ago now, it was. Polite as an angel is that little fellow," smiled the blacksmith fondly. "Brought me the wax mould one day and came to collect the copy the next. *"That lisp will soon disappear*, I said to him – *don't you worry. Just wait until your new front teeth come through."*

Chapter 25

A Fine Figure of a Man

Sir Percy FitzNigel trotted down the narrow track between sunny banks of sweet tansy, breathing in its lemony scent and surprising a small herd of deer foraging in the lane. Fustian followed behind, coughing on his barrel-chested pony, its wide panniers squeezing between swathes of cow parsley and marjoram, sending clouds of seeds billowing into the drowsy air.

"So," brayed Percy merrily over his shoulder, "a murder at Saint Wilfred's eh? Couldn't be better! Thank heavens I decided to come down early. And quite a coincidence as it happens. The Archbishop's already had a word in my ear about that place. *'FitzNigel,'* he said to me, slapping me on the back, *'take a glance over the abbey for me while you're there. Write me a report.'* There are rumours, you know, Fustian, and the Arch B doesn't like it: gluttony, drunkenness, monks wandering the moors and woods poaching and carousing with the local wenches!" He pushed aside a beech branch, heavy with hairy nutshells, waited until Fustian was almost level, then let it spring back in his face, hooting with glee as Fustian tumbled backwards into the rutted lane. "Ooops a daisy," he snorted. "We'll make a horseman of you yet, Fustian!"

"Pompous little upstart," hissed Fustian, prising himself out of a deep rut and shaking his fist in the direction of Percy's willowy waist.

"What was that, Fustian?" called Percy suspiciously, lips curling back from his horsy teeth.

"You must teach me the art, Sir Percy," said his servant, dipping an obsequious bow and scrambling back amongst the cushions on Griselda's sagging saddle.

Sir Percy frowned. He could never quite trust Fustian – something insolent in his manner – but the ruffian would have to do until the King promoted him to Chief Justice. Maybe then he could stretch to tuppence a day.

"Yeees," drawled Percy as they emerged from the lane into a field of uncut wheat, "those monks seem to have forgotten what they're here for – to pray for the souls of people like me who are too busy to pray for themselves. Take old King Richard for instance. The monks are still doing penance for him and he's been dead for years!"

They had made good speed from *The Pious Pilgrim*, rising early and on the hard road by daybreak and now by mid-afternoon the stubble plains were giving way to heather hills, rising in purple folds from the valley of the River Twist. The sky was a cloudless blue as they turned their backs on the dense dark forest and began to descend into the fertile valley. A mile or so off in the distance, they could just make out the yellow monastery of Saint Wilfred, dominated by its massive Norman tower and defensive gatehouse. Sir Percy FitzNigel glanced nervously over his shoulder into the tangle of forest trees. But it was an idyllic afternoon – hard to imagine robbers and bandits amongst the heady fumes of poppies and the corn buntings' tinny song.

"What shall we talk about now, Fustian?" said Sir Percy. "How about horsemanship? Now, you're in an ideal position to learn something today whilst you're riding behind me. Just watch my seat! There's nobody that can rival me in the handling of a horse, hunting, hawking, swordsmanship … are you paying attention, Fustian?"

"Er yes, Sir Percy," he said pulling a well worn acorn out of his ear, "every last syllable!"

There was a sudden rustle at the forest's edge. Sir Percy's chestnut horse shied slightly, but trotted on. "What was that, Fustian?" said Percy sharply.

"Dunno sir. Pheasant maybe, or a woodcock."

Percy shuddered. It was definitely a touch cooler now in the shadow of the forest. He reached for his deerskin cloak. "I must admit I'm looking forward to seeing Sir Ranulf de Lacy again – a fine figure of a man, with as rare a wine cellar as any Baron in these parts. We'll fit in some hunting – spear a wild boar or two each, no trouble at all. Hah, some people say they're too dangerous to hunt without a pack of hounds and yet Percy FitzNigel, with his simple bow and arrow, is a match for the meanest beast in the county."

It was upon him before Sir Percy even saw it, foaming

at the tusks, its ears erect. Hairy hackles bristling with fury, the huge boar charged at Sir Percy's horse. Rearing in panic, eyes rolling to the whites, the terrified mare flung Sir Percy FitzNigel screaming from the saddle. Without so much as a backward glance, Fustian trotted past, leaving Sir Percy to his fate, whimpering in terror, crawling in the undergrowth, beseeching God to save his skin. Brave Sir Percy made no attempt to draw the dagger at his belt as he scrambled, sobbing for the cover of a nearby tree, his emerald hose torn at the knees and his hands bleeding. Perhaps it was the smell of Percy's blood that goaded the beast to madness, or maybe the fearful whinnying of the lawyer's frightened horse. Whatever the cause, the powerful animal charged again, spearing Sir Percy's hose at their tightest point, on the smooth round curve of his neat little bottom.

Percy's wild screams were suddenly drowned by the pounding of charging hooves and the sharp high horn of a hunter as a mounted figure came thundering through the forest in a welter of baying hounds, his spear held high in his right hand, the reins of his powerful mount in his left. With a blood curdling roar, the boar spun round to face Sir Ranulf de Lacy. The old soldier's charger reared but the baron held his seat, thrusting his spear deep into the boar's chest as his horse's hooves came pounding down, narrowly missing Sir Percy FitzNigel, as he cowered at the bottom of a tree, the stain on his emerald hose spreading like scarlet ink.

Chapter 26

Micklow Manor

S ir Ranulf de Lacy was a widower. Thirty summers had bloomed and withered since his dear wife Rosamunde had died in childbed leaving a motherless daughter for his comfort. He had called the baby Alice. Micklow Manor, with its deer parks bristling with stag and wild pigs, had been in his family for generations, a gift from a grateful King to Sir Ranulf's ancestor who had fought in the First Crusade. It was a sprawling, fortified country house, well suited to the present Sir Ranulf, himself a hardened campaigner for the cross, who now in his sixtieth year had exchanged his war horse for a hunter and his shield and crossbow for a well-honed boar spear.

It was evening. The moon was rising over the dusky battlements. Owls hooted in the hazel groves and bats chased glistening beetles in the balmy air. The rare glass windows of the turreted manor were ablaze with candles, casting dancing fireflies of light on the cool pike pools of the ornamental gardens – for Sir Ranulf de Lacy, Baron of Micklow Manor, was entertaining the King's Justice.

Sir Percy FitzNigel was feeling uncomfortable. It was painful to sit down, even on the softest goose feather cushion, and besides, he could swear that the boar's head was glaring spitefully at him with its mean little eyes as it lay on the silver platter in the dining hall.

"So, Sir Percy," chortled the baron, spearing a piece of roasted goat on his hunting knife and offering it to the hawk on his shoulder. He still wore his bloodstained riding britches. "You've had a taste of our fine hunting country already! Now serve yourself, why don't you? How about a slice of our tusked friend over there? Lord, if I hadn't galloped up in the nick of time it would have been Percy on the platter and the hog sitting next to me with a napkin around its neck!"

Sir Ranulf smiled mischievously as he sliced into a juicy piglet, hot fat spattering his tunic. Sir Percy twitched, shooting a malevolent glance at the Baron.

"Hardly a likely outcome, Sir Ranulf," he said, pretending to laugh. "I was merely gathering my strength after rescuing my servant from the ferocious swine when you happened upon me. I'd sent Fustian on his way unscathed and was reaching for my own dagger when you stole the prize! It's not that I blame you, Sir Ranulf. I'd brought the beast to bay for you and I was more than happy to allow you the pleasure of finishing him off. I'll say this for you though," he added generously, "you did pretty well for a man of your age. But you must agree that it's a young man's sport when all is said and done."

Sir Ranulf's eyes twinkled as he twisted the hairs in his broad nostrils. His nose was almost flat – the result of a quarrel with his helmet and a Saracen warrior in the Holy Land.

"Grateful for your assistance, FitzNigel," he nodded, chuckling inwardly and following Sir Percy's gaze towards his hunting trophies, mounted on the walls. "Just a selection of my triumphs," drawled Sir Ranulf. "Edible on the left – stag, hare, boar – and vermin on the right – wolf, otter, badger, fox – only thing missing is a unicorn but I still live in hope. Need a young virgin to entrap it, you see," he laughed, "and I've never persuaded one to come along with me!" He glanced wickedly at Sir Percy, willing him to take the bait.

Sir Percy reached for a heron's egg and tossed it arrogantly into his mouth, eyeing his reflection in the pewter tankard as he chewed. "Look no further, Sir Ranulf," he preened, puffing out his chest and wincing only slightly at the pain in his buttock. The French wine on an empty stomach was having a numbing effect. "If you need any advice about cutting a dash with the ladies, Percy FitzNigel's the name!"

Sir Ranulf raised an enigmatic brow. He was beginning to grow weary of this insufferable popinjay and the night was still young. "The Chief Justice is indisposed, you say?" he sighed regretfully. "Pity. I was looking forward to a visit from my old friend Sir Henry …"

"Yees," simpered Percy, "his health's crumbling, poor old boy. But what can you expect when you grow as long in the tusk as him," he shrugged, glancing towards the boar's head which didn't seem to be glaring anymore. "Must be pushing sixty by now."

Sir Ranulf de Lacy snorted into his tankard. He glanced apologetically at the boar, wishing he could make amends for slitting the wrong throat.

"So Sir Ranulf," said Percy, refilling his tankard, "have you seen the Sheriff lately? What sport do we have for the assizes? I was relieved to hear about the Saint Wilfred's murder. Last time I came down with Sir Henry, nobody's neck was stretched."

Sir Ranulf snapped his fingers irritably at a servant who was hovering in the shadows. "Another jug of claret, Martin," he rapped. "Make it a big one, there's a good fellow."

"Biggest one I can find, Sir," winked the servant, scurrying off.

"I did happen to see the Sheriff yesterday, since you ask," said Sir Ranulf. "I understand a moneylender from the town has been arrested already, so there won't be much work for you there. I can't say he'll have a fair trial before the townspeople of Saint Agnes though, poor fellow. I expect you'll have heard of the unrest against the Jews hereabouts, Sir Percy – hounded from their homes and their dwellings burnt to the ground."

"Indeed I have, Baron," replied Percy, mistaking Sir Ranulf's tone. "Serves the vermin right, I say! We have the same problems with the greedy parasites in London, wailing in their synagogues and growing fat at the expense of God-fearing Christians. No more Crusades against the Muslim infidels, I say, until we've settled a few feuds with the Jewish heathens in our midst."

"I can hardly agree," replied Sir Ranulf coldly. "If it were not for the Jewish moneylenders, Christian Kings could not raise armies, or merchants embark on trading. People are happy enough to borrow money from the Jews when it suits them and then make them into scapegoats as soon as things go wrong. I have no doubt the foolish people of Saint Agnes believe what they are told – that the Jews have forked tails in their britches and horns under their hats."

Sir Percy FitzNigel was frowning foolishly, his large front teeth protruding over his bottom lip. *What curious opinions the old baron held. Too many blows to the head in the Holy Land, perhaps.* "Well, I'm pleased to hear the culprit has already been found since I've been entrusted with a mission of the greatest importance for the Archbishop. He wants a report on Saint Wilfred's Abbey for the new King. He wants to know what old Theodore was up to – letting the monks run riot, so I'm told. Very good news that the old abbot has gone to meet his maker, I say. Leaves the way clear to put a better man at the helm."

Sir Ranulf's face was stony, his hand hovering around the dagger at his waist. He was fighting down an overwhelming desire to teach this pompous upstart a lesson. "You will remember, Sir Percy, whilst you are a guest in my house," he said softly, his voice as cold as the steel at his fingertips, "that Abbot Theodore was one of my dearest friends – a man of tremendous courage and a compassionate soldier."

But Percy FitzNigel was unabashed. By now the fine claret was coursing through his veins. With a belch of satisfaction, towards the ceiling for good manners' sake, he got up from the table and began to pace the room unsteadily. He posed theatrically in the candle light as he examined Sir Ranulf's possessions with the air of a connoisseur – fine tapestries and mementos of the baron's soldiering days – when his eyes fell upon a dusty harp in the corner of the hall. With a hoot of delight he pranced up to the instrument and began to pluck ineptly at the strings, twanging a discord. "There's no musical instrument known to man at which Sir Percy FitzNigel does not surpass his peers," he slurred. "No ballad ever written …"

"Put that down this instant!" boomed Sir Ranulf rising, "before I slit you from the navel to the neck!"

Sir Percy FitzNigel leapt back with a shriek of surprise. He glared at Sir Ranulf in drunken indignation. "I humbly beg your pardon," he mumbled in an offended tone.

Sir Ranulf's hand dropped to his side, the dagger still in his belt. He sank down heavily at the table, breathing hard, ashamed of his momentary loss of control. After all, what could this dull-witted buffoon know of the painful estrangement between his daughter and himself?

"I beg your pardon for speaking in haste, Sir Percy," he said quietly. "The harp belonged to my daughter … a long time ago."

But Sir Ranulf's humble apology was wasted on Sir Percy. Relieved at the baron's sudden change of tone, he reeled back to the table, reaching for his tankard of wine.

"No offence taken," he brayed, insensitive to the last. He leaned across the roasted piglet confidentially, as if Sir Ranulf were an old and trusted friend. "Now just remind me," he said with a familiar wink. "Isn't she the young filly that married the old miller? Damned funny business, I always thought. What in the world possessed a noblewoman like her to choose to sink so low?"

Chapter 27

A Tangled Web

An owl flew silently from the hazel groves of Micklow Manor, down the winding silver ribbon of the River Twist, towards the warm glow of the candlelit abbey. The boys' shrill plainsong rose like a cloud of incense into the shadowy vault as Prior Solomon congratulated himself on a second complete day of services. It was Vespers, the service of the evening star. All the lamps were lit, casting a dim flickering light over the painted saints on the walls and the fine carvings in the choir.

Tom and Herbert hesitated outside the south door of the abbey. They'd searched everywhere for Ed for most of the afternoon. No sign of the little wretch – and now they were late. With any luck they'd catch up with him after Vespers.

The singing straggled to a halt in a fumble of music books. The octomanipulator had run into a touch of trouble. Brother Ethelwig sidled into the choir stalls with a pair of pincers and a small jug of walnut oil. Prior Solomon's face was aloof. Only the tiniest twitch of his eye and a soft intake of breath betrayed his irritation. Things would soon improve – once the elections were over. If Brother Ethelwig refused to fall into line then he would have no choice but to find him a place elsewhere. The prior compressed his lips as Ethelwig squeezed between the choristers, oiling the creaking joints of the retractable arms.

"Ooops, sorry Edmund," he apologised, crushing toes as he sidled along the row. A rich nutty smell mingled pleasantly with the aroma of beeswax candles. "That should do the trick," he said hopefully.

Prior Solomon's distant gaze followed Ethelwig as he scuttled back to his place. He flicked an invisible speck of dust from his sleeve as he turned expectantly back to the choir. *God in heaven – what now?* Two novices were creeping into the chapel, trying not to be noticed. Prior Solomon's patience was wearing thin. *Brother Herbert should lose some weight if he wants to hide behind pillars. And does Brother Thomas really suppose he is unobserved?*

The choir started singing again but it was a ragged sound without Brother Fergus and his energetic baton. It made Tom feel hollow inside. He scanned the first row of the choir, searching for Edmund's round face. There it was. A moon of innocence in the flickering amber light, intent on catching nobody's eye, least of all Tom's.

"There's Ed, the little devil!" hissed Tom. "Next to Odo – behind the music stands. We'll grab him as they're filing out in case he tries to give us the slip again."

Prior Solomon was intoning the final prayers and Tom was preparing to dart from his pew as soon as the choir began to move, when Herbert grabbed his arm. "I don't believe it! Ed's disappeared!"

Tom blinked. The space in the choir where Edmund had stood was empty.

Tom and Herbert raced into the sacristy passage ignoring the indignant voice of Brother Dunstan calling them back.

"Where now?" mouthed Herbert.

Tom put his finger to his lips. "Shh. Listen." There was a faint creak from the direction of the sacristy. Tom jerked his head towards the sound, pulling Herbert behind him.

The sacristy was gloomy, with only a small round window, high up in the rear wall; an inky circle, peppered with stars. On the left hand side stood the famous cupboard, a large iron padlock hanging askew on its broad linked chain. Set into the back wall was the bread oven – a disused relic from days gone by, when the sacrist used to bake the holy wafers every day. All was silent.

Herbert scoured the room with his eyes. "The oven," he mouthed to Tom, who was already on his way, creeping across the tiled floor like a thief in the night. With a groan of rusty hinges, Tom flung wide the door to reveal a small sooty boy, crouching in the dark; his thin grey robe rucked up around his knobbly knees.

"You!" snarled Tom, reaching in and grabbing a bunch of Ed's robe in his hand. "What the devil have you been up to?" Edmund shrank back against the bricks with a startled cry, squeezing his eyes tight shut. "*You've* got some explaining to do," Tom hissed through gritted teeth, "and you're going to start right now!"

"Why have you been avoiding us?" asked Herbert more gently.

"Did you think we wouldn't catch up with you, you little liar!" spat Tom. "Why did you go to the blacksmith's forge to have a key made? Who put you up to it?"

"Give him a chance, Tom," said Herbert. "Let him get out of the oven."

Ed scrambled out, wiping his eyes on his sleeve. He stood awkwardly in front of the two boys on the cool tiled floor, staring at his sandals.

Tom took a deep breath. "Look Ed. You've done a terrible thing. Brother Fergus is rotting in gaol accused of pawning the sacristy treasure and keeping the money for himself. He's going to London tomorrow to face the church court at Westminster. If he's found guilty, he'll be stripped of his robes, his reputation, everything – and he'll never come back here again."

Edmund looked up at Tom with terrified eyes. His nose was running.

"Tom's right, Ed," said Herbert. "If you're protecting somebody, then you'd better tell us right now."

"You won't believe me even if I tell you," wailed Edmund, bursting into tears at last. "I didn't want to do it, but he threatened me. He said bad things would happen if I didn't do it – that I'd be sent away – and I've got nowhere to go. I'm a real orphan, not like you and Herbert."

Herbert crouched down on the floor and put his arm

around Edmund. "Come on, Ed. We're your friends. We'll help you. Just tell us his name."

Edmund gazed despairingly at Tom, his hand over his mouth, as if more than anything in the world he wanted to stop his words from tumbling out.

"All right," he said at last in a defeated tone. "If you stop bullying me, I'll tell you."

Tom took a step back and folded his arms. Edmund straightened his shoulders with a determined sniff.

"It was Brother Fergus who made me do it!" he blurted suddenly. "It's not what you wanted to hear is it? But it's the truth."

August 5th 1220

Chapter 28

A Hard and Heavy Punishment

The summer mist lay like a gauzy veil across the garden of Tirley Grange. Bessie breathed in the cool dawn air and hugged her cloak about her more closely. She had slept badly, her night a tangle of confused dreams: *Abigail trembling on the scaffold, a noose around her neck, a packet of love letters clutched tightly in her hand ... her own mother in the jeering crowd, arm in arm with Brother Benedict.* A magpie cackled in the blackthorn. "One for sorrow..." whispered Bessie, kissing her fingers towards the bird to ward off ill-luck.

She had woken with a deep sense of foreboding. It had been growing stronger ever since Gabriel Miller had burst into the kitchen last evening with the news that the King's Justice had arrived in the town.

"*He's staying up at Micklow Manor with your father, my dear,*" he had muttered, in an undertone to his wife.

Alice Miller glanced sharply at her husband, her colour

deepening. *"No doubt Sir Ranulf will enjoy the company,"* she said, breaking off her embroidery thread with a snap. *"He and Sir Henry de Mandeville are old friends."*

"Sir Henry is indisposed, I understand," said Gabriel. *"They have sent that prancing peacock that came for the last assizes – Fitz somebody or other."*

Alice caught her breath. *"Well Sir Ranulf is welcome to him,"* she murmured, glancing uneasily at Bessie, *"but this is ill news for Eli Abrahams. Sir Henry tempered justice with mercy, but that swaggering upstart knows no pity, if my memory serves me right."*

Now, as the sun's early rays glinted on the spiders' webs under the brambles, Bessie had made up her mind. She could no longer bear to sit fretting at Tirley Grange waiting for news of Abigail to come to her. She would return to the town and find out for herself what was happening, whatever the risk from the constable's dog or her father's birch switch cane. Besides, she had other business in Saint Agnes too, she told herself. The little matter of the Hebrew word at the bottom of the bonds she and Abbi had discovered in Eli's house. Maybe she could snare two birds in one net – find out news of Abigail and obtain a Hebrew translation at the same time.

Golden patches of morning light mocked the damp walls of Abigail's cold cell. She could almost touch her father's feet – if she stretched her toes just a fraction more – but the manacles had bitten into her thin ankles and there was little flesh now between the rusty iron and the bone beneath the skin.

"Father," she hissed urgently. She touched his foot with a groan of pain and a stab of regret at waking him. Eli Abrahams opened his eyes, wondering at the pins and needles in his hands.

"The King's Justice is here, Father," she said, frowning at his hacking cough. "I heard the town constable talking to the watchman outside. So at least there'll be a proper trial now." There were flecks of blood on her father's lips.

Eli flexed his hands in their chains, struggling to wipe his mouth on his shoulder. "A fair trial?" he wheezed with a bitter laugh. "For a Jew?" He shook his head sadly. "No Abigail. You are deceiving yourself."

"But surely someone will give evidence for you. Bessie Miller, perhaps. She came to our house, remember – on the night Brother Benedict was murdered. Bessie will tell the truth … and what about the Rabbi? The Rabbi would surely speak of your good character," she said, trying to sound hopeful. Eli's eyes were oddly bright, glittering with a feverish heat. In spite of the coolness of the prison cell, his face was bathed in sweat. Abigail turned away, hiding the tears in her eyes.

"The Rabbi?" he said, an eyebrow raised in gentle mockery. "These people have no more respect for the Rabbi than they do for me. How can I submit to a trial on a trumped-up charge in front of the townspeople who murdered my wife? No, my dear," he said firmly. "I am resolved."

"R … resolved …?" she choked, an icy hand around her throat. "What do you mean?"

"I will refuse this new kind of trial, Abigail. I will not allow them the satisfaction of their pitiful charade."

Abigail stared at her father in horror. "No father," she gasped as the full meaning of his words froze her blood. "You know what they do to people who refuse a jury trial! And what will happen to me?" she wailed.

"I trust the King's Justice will set you free, my dear," said Eli, with a weak smile that belied the fear in his eyes. "After all, it is only the spite of the town constable that keeps you here. The Justice will surely see that you have done no wrong, whatever lies he believes of me."

But Abigail was screaming inside. She wanted to howl and weep, fall at his feet and beg him to change his mind, but she was chained to the wall, and besides, the despair in her heart was beyond tears.

The Jewish synagogue was as mournful as a prison with its narrow loopholes by way of windows and a door so low it seemed to beg pardon for being there at all. It squatted at the end of a filthy passage in the dingiest part of Saint Agnes. Bessie's face felt hot under her woollen hood as she rounded the corner into Heathen Street. She paused uncertainly at the synagogue, the scrap of parchment bearing the mysterious Hebrew word clutched in her hand. With a hasty backward glance down the dusty alley, she tapped on the low lintel.

There was no reply, but intuition told her someone was listening on the other side of the door. She put her lips to the rough wood. "I'm a friend of Abigail Abrahams," she called softly. "Please open up if there's anybody there."

A chink of candlelight glimmered at the edge of the door. It opened just a slice, enough for her to slip unseen into the lamp-lit darkness. The Rabbi raised a curious lamp to Bessie's face, tiny flames dancing in his eyes. His face was sharp, deep grooves running between his thin nostrils and the corners of his mouth – a stern face, scholarly but not unkind.

"It is not often that I have the pleasure of seeing a Christian in Heathen Street," he said with a hint of bitterness, setting the lantern down on a table. He motioned Bessie towards a low stool. "But I know you to be a friend of Abigail Abrahams," he added more gently. "I have seen you in the marketplace. May I ask why you have come?"

Bessie sat down heavily, her eyes searching the shadows for inspiration. *What am I doing here?* she thought, hopelessly. *After all, what can a simple girl like me do for Abigail now?* She felt suddenly foolish, clumsy and out of place.

"I know you bear us no malice," said the Rabbi, "but these are troubled times, my dear. What can a Christian child want with a Rabbi?"

"I have come to ask for news of Eli Abrahams and his daughter," she said humbly. "There's no one else I can ask. He will never have a fair trial before the assizes. No one will dare to speak up for him, even if they wanted to, but I know he's done no wrong. I saw him on the night of the murder." She gazed wretchedly at the Rabbi. "But who would listen to a girl like me?"

The Rabbi studied Bessie's face in silence, a curious expression in his eyes – reluctant respect, mingled with regret. "You have a kind heart for a Christian," he said slowly, "but things are worse than you fear. Clearly you have not heard the news – but then, how could you? I have only just learned of it myself – on my way to the synagogue this morning."

"What news?" breathed Bessie in alarm.

The Rabbi's face was grave. "Eli Abrahams is refusing trial by jury," he replied, holding her gaze. "And there is only one alternative for a man who refuses to be judged by his peers."

Bessie's mouth was dry and there was a sour taste on her tongue.

"Peine forte et dure," said the Rabbi, his eyes like stones. "Heavy and hard punishment. If the justices believe him to be guilty and he refuses to be tried, they will tie him to the floor with a plank across his chest. And then they will pile heavy rocks on the plank until he agrees to the trial … or is slowly crushed to death."

Bessie sprang to her feet with a cry. The room spun round as the blood drained from her face. She was seized by an overwhelming urge to get away from the synagogue – to run through the sunlit fields back home to Tirley Grange. But that would be cowardly, she told herself, closing her eyes and screwing her courage. She clutched at the Rabbi's sleeve with a beseeching sob.

"But surely there's something you can do for them!" she begged.

But the Rabbi's face was grim. He placed his veined hand over hers and pressed it kindly. "You know as well as I that I cannot help Eli Abrahams," he said, with a shake of his head. "You cannot believe that the King's Justice would hear the pleas of a hated Jew. But perhaps there is something else that I can do for you," he said gently, his eyes straying to the parchment in Bessie's hand.

She stared at the scrap of writing through a shimmering mist, almost as if she had forgotten about the mysterious Hebrew word. A tear rolled down her cheek as she held it out uncertainly to the old Rabbi.

He raised the parchment to the lantern flame, narrowing his eyes. "This is the Hebrew word for 'stranger'," he said in surprise. "That is what my people are, my dear. Strangers. Wanderers in a foreign land."

Chapter 29

A Cloud of Dust

The outer court of the abbey was oddly busy; everyone with a pressing reason to be 'just passing through': a forgotten chisel, an urgent need for a jug of milk from the dairy. For the rumour had bustled through the abbey – Prior Solomon was banishing Brother Fergus to London – and the courtyard was a bubbling cauldron of gossip, as ill-nature rubbed shoulders with pity to witness his departure in disgrace.

Two buzzards soared in wide circles above the abbey, scanning the ground for prey. Tom shielded his eyes from the blistering sun, strangely chilled by the birds' melancholy cry. He passed his hand over his face as if to wipe away his expression of despair. He could hear the voice of Brother Ambrose floating from the quillery window, delivering a lesson on the correct mixture of iron salts and vinegar for the perfect tawny ink. But if Tom had peeped inside, he would have seen that Brother Edmund was not in his seat.

His owl feather quill lay abandoned on his sloping desk.

Herbert sat on a low wall, irritating an ants' nest with a stick. "I still can't believe it. You can't trust anybody. To think of Brother Fergus threatening poor Ed."

Tom shook his head. "You can think what you like. I don't believe it!" he said, his voice trembling. He screwed up his eyes. *It can't be true!* he told himself for the hundredth time, fighting down the niggling worm of a doubt. "Brother Fergus already had a key to the sacristy," he said, his chin raised in defiance. "Why should he need another one?"

"To give to somebody else, maybe?" said Herbert.

Tom twisted his mouth in scorn. "It's not in his nature," he snapped. "There's never been a better monk at Saint Wilfred's. But I'll tell you something, Herbert. I'm going to have this out with Ed after his quill lesson. There's more to this than meets the eye. I know it!"

But Ed was not in the quillery. He was hiding in a cool corner of the north cloister, listening to the rumpus in the outer court and the mournful tolling of the abbey bell. He hugged his knees to his chin, wet face buried in his robe, inhaling the musty smell of damp fabric. Stuffing his fingers in his ears, he rocked himself to and fro like a baby.

Tom caught his breath. Brother Fergus was emerging from a passageway into the outer court, flanked by the gaoler and Brother Dunstan, with Mungo yelping plaintively by their side. The sacrist blinked like a bewildered mole, eyes dazzled by the unfamiliar sun. His unruly ginger hair lacked its usual energy and his habit hung limply about his knees. He stooped clumsily to calm the leaping dog but his trembling hands were bound. Straightening up, he gazed around the yard, his eyes red-rimmed, perplexed. "I … I am at a loss tae understand …" he stumbled. "Why should I pawn the monastery treasure? It was my sacred trust …"

The novice master silenced him with a wave of his hand as he handed a bulging purse of coin to the two young monks in travelling clothes who were adjusting the saddles of their horses. "You have miscalculated, Fergus," he snapped. "You thought that your popularity would protect you from blame. But Novice Edmund has confessed about the duplicate key."

"Novice Edmund?" exclaimed the sacrist with a bitter laugh.

His eyes scanned the crowd as if searching for a friendly face. Harnesses jangled; the escorts keen to be gone. Tom's hands tightened into fists. He gazed back at Brother Fergus in misery, tears welling in his eyes. He bent down and pretended to fiddle with his sandal, wiping his face on his robe so that Herbert wouldn't see. He didn't notice Bessie Miller, waving frantically to him from the back of the crowd, her face bright red with running from the town.

Up in his study on the south side of the abbey, Prior Solomon's dark head was bent over his desk, his quill scurrying decisively over the velvet parchment. He was composing a report on Saint Wilfred's Abbey for the King's Justice to deliver to the Bishop in London. He had to make haste for Percy FitzNigel was to take a dish of eggs with him at mid-day and the servants were busy preparing the

Abbot's private dining hall. He had filled one page already with a catalogue of misdeeds and a list of proposed reforms. He pulled his long nose. The incessant tolling of the abbey bell was disturbing the delicate rhythm of his thoughts. He dipped his swan feather quill into the coloured acid with a dismissive shake of his head. He could not allow himself the luxury of regrets. The abbey would be a better place without the likes of Brother Fergus, he assured himself; the surrender of a diseased limb for the greater health of the rest of the body.

He laid his quill carefully in his oriental writing casket. Softening some sealing wax in the candle flame, he let the sticky fluid drip onto the thick sheets of folded yellow parchment. If this document had the desired effect, he would be using the abbot's seal before the turning leaves began to fall. He was not relishing the prospect of Sir Percy's visit, but if the Justice had the ear of the Bishop, then Prior Solomon must have the ear of the Justice. He must take care to make the right impression on Sir Percy – swallow his pride and woo the conceited puppy to his side.

Down in the shadowy cloisters Edmund's heart beat fast. A veil of confusion was lifting from his eyes. *I don't have to do this,* he thought fiercely. *I don't care what he does to me – I can't live with myself if I let this happen. If I don't speak up now – I'll hate myself forever.*

He sprang decisively to his feet, tripping over his robe and smashing his hand against a rough pillar. He was glad of the pain. It was no more than he deserved. He raced across the cloisters, past the sparkling fountain and into the cool cellarium, ripe with the tang of maturing cheese. He burst into the outer court, staring wildly around. Mungo was howling in anguish, straining at the rope that tethered him to the bridle post. Edmund gazed down the beaten track in horror. But all that remained at the empty bend in the road was a small cloud of dust. Brother Fergus had gone! Whirling round, searching the thinning crowd for any sign of his friends, he felt a hand on his shoulder.

"Listen to me, Ed," hissed Tom through his teeth. "I don't believe a word you told us last night. You're coming up to the Swallows' Nest for a little chat with me – and you won't be going down again until you've told me the truth!"

Chapter 30

Wanderer in a Foreign Land

As Prior Solomon strode resolutely towards the abbot's dining hall, Sir Percy FitzNigel was trotting gingerly towards the abbey, a soft feather bolster plumped around his injured buttock.

"Come along, Fustian," he called, twisting delicately in the saddle. "Slept in the dog kennel all right?"

"As if you care!" huffed Fustian, more dilapidated than ever in the bright morning sun.

"Didn't quite catch that, Fustian."

"I said *'with room to spare'*, Sir Percy," replied the faded servant with a mournful droop of his shoulders.

"Cheer up, you miserable mule. I was feeling a bit down in the mouth myself this morning but this news about the old Jew has raised my spirits no end. I've never watched anybody being pressed to death before. The thought has given me quite an appetite!"

Up in the Swallows' Nest, Edmund tried to struggle, but Tom wouldn't let go of his shoulders. "What?" he exploded. "Say that again!"

"P ... Prior Solomon asked me to get the key made! It ... it wasn't Brother Fergus at all," Ed stammered, bursting into tears. "He told me he'd throw me out of the abbey if I told anybody about it. I only lied because I didn't want to be sent away – but now it's too late," he wailed. "Brother Fergus has gone!"

"We know that, you little devil," hissed Tom. "Why did Prior Solomon want the key anyway? Come on Ed. Answer!" he shouted, shaking Ed roughly by the arm.

"Stop it, Tom," cried Herbert. "You'll hurt him."

"How should I know?" sobbed Ed, wiping his streaming nose with the back of his hand. "Why should he tell me?"

Tom threw up his hands in despair. "Come on Herbert! Think! Why would Prior Solomon want the key to the sacristy?" He paused, his face creased in concentration. "Presumably to steal the treasure and pawn it to Eli Abrahams!" he said, answering his own question. "But why? What did he need money for?"

Tom's mind was spinning: *What was going on? Was Ed telling the truth this time? Maybe Eli Abrahams had known about Prior Solomon and the key all along. But the moneylender was locked in gaol where he couldn't tell anyone. How very convenient for the prior! And Brother Fergus was a perfect scapegoat. His job as sacrist made him look like the thief – and Prior Solomon had let him take the blame and frightened poor Ed into silence. And what, if anything, had this to do with Brother Benedict?*

"I can't work it out," groaned Tom aloud, clutching his head. He spun round as Bessie clambered over the parapet in a shiver of ivy.

"I thought I'd find you here!" she burst out. "Didn't you see me in the outer court? Eli Abrahams is refusing jury trial. They're going to press him to death with heavy stones tomorrow morning! You've got to talk to Ethelwig. If he's protecting Job Pug, you must persuade him to tell what he knows before it's too late…!"

"Wait, Bessie," interrupted Tom. "Just calm down! We've some news of our own. It seems Brother Fergus is innocent after all! Ed's told us Prior Solomon had a duplicate key made for the sacristy cupboard behind Fergus's back!"

Bessie gave a start. "I've some news about the abbey treasure myself. I asked the Rabbi about the Hebrew word we found at the bottom of the ledgers I took from Eli's house. The word means *stranger. Wanderer in a foreign land.*"

Tom whistled through his teeth. "Wanderer in a foreign land?"

"That's what the Jews are," shrugged Bessie. "So the Rabbi said – wanderers without a home. But I don't think it helps much …"

"Oh yes it does, Bessie," said Tom, looking pointedly at Herbert. "Don't you see? It could apply just as well to Prior Solomon. You know – a stranger – a foreigner. Maybe the prior went to Eli in disguise. Perhaps all Eli knew was that the person bringing the abbey treasure was a foreigner. Even after all these years, Prior Solomon still doesn't speak like us."

"But it's too late now," groaned Herbert. "Brother Fergus has been sent to London for trial. And who would take Ed's word against the prior's anyway – assuming he's telling the truth at last?"

"It's never too late," said Tom, his eyes flashing. "But we must have more evidence. We need to search the prior's room. See if we can find anything – any clue as to what he's been up to. He's expecting the King's Justice this morning. He's taken over the abbot's own dining hall. And that suits us perfectly."

"But Tom!" cried Bessie. "What about Eli? The King's Justice is already here! It's the assizes tomorrow. If you go chasing off to the prior's room looking for clues about the sacristy treasure you're wasting precious time. I need you to talk to Ethelwig *now* – ask him questions about Job. That's more important than Brother Fergus at the moment!"

Tom glared back at her, a stubborn look in his eye. "I know we're short of time, Bessie, but this might be our only chance of getting into the prior's room. I haven't forgotten about Ethelwig, but I have to do this first. I'll go and see him straight after – I promise. Come on, Herbert. We've got to be quick."

"Can I come too?" said Ed in a small voice.

"No," said Tom coldly. "The fewer the better." Ed shrank back, crestfallen. Tom felt a sudden surge of pity. "All right, Ed," he said, softening a little. "You can't come to the prior's room – but you can join us later. Stay here until the sun is over the tower, and then meet us outside Ethelwig's room. Come on, Herbert! We've very little time, and I need you to stand guard."

Chapter 31

Blackmail

The abbot's house lay on the bank of the river, between the novices' dormitory and the infirmary – a little too close to Prior Solomon's study for the comfort of the two boys, who were holding their breath under the dining hall window.

"You and I have a great deal in common, Prior," came Sir Percy's high pitched hoot from the casement above Tom's head. "Both men of ambition in our different ways."

"Prior Solomon's bound to have locked his door," whispered Tom. "I'm going in through the back window. You hang around here with your ears pinned back and give me a shout if anyone comes."

"All right," swallowed Herbert. "But hurry! I've got a bad feeling about this."

Tom scrambled over the stone sill of Prior Solomon's study and dropped down behind the horn shutters. An incense burner was still smouldering, spirals of fragrant smoke snaking into the still air. He gazed around the room at Prior Solomon's exotic possessions: a water clock in the shape of a lion, an inlaid writing chest on a low table by the hearth.

Tom crouched down by the bed and peered underneath. Nothing more suspicious than a pair of silken slippers. Turning to the small shelf of books, he selected each in turn, feeling along between the bindings and the rough wall behind for any sign of a key. He hurried over to the writing chest with an anxious glance at the door.

There was a drawer in the front with a handle in the shape of a crescent moon. Tom pulled and twisted in vain. He lifted the patterned lid and peered inside at the delicate brushes, sharp knives and pots of bright ink. He ran his finger along the hopscotch design of chequered ebony and ivory that wound its way around the rim, stopping as his nail snagged on a lozenge of polished wood that stood slightly proud of the intricate design. With the faintest ping the draw slid open.

Sir Percy FitzNigel drained the last drop of wine from his silver goblet at the abbot's table, stifling a belch. "Now don't lose any sleep over the position of abbot, Prior Solomon," he said with a familiar wink. "I'll have a word with the Arch B just as soon as I return to London. He relies on me. If *I* say you're the right man for the job, he'll fix the election, don't you worry. It was too bad about the murder of your bursar but that small inconvenience will be cleared up before the sun sets tomorrow, I can promise you that. Have you seen the pile of stones in the market square?"

Prior Solomon coughed, concealing his dislike beneath the charade of a wayward crumb. It was time to send this conceited puppy on his way.

"I am grateful for your good opinion," he replied, rising from the table. "So if you would care to step along to my study, I will give you the report on the reforms I propose. It is already sealed, so I need detain you no longer. No doubt you have more *pressing* matters to attend to than the affairs of our humble abbey …"

Sir Percy flung back his head and chortled in delight at the prior's inadvertent pun. He closed his eyes in comradely merriment, but when he opened them again, Prior Solomon was already through the door and leading the way down the stairs.

Alone in Prior Solomon's study, Tom was shaking. In his left hand he held a dull black key, its fob in the shape of a chalice – identical in every way to the one that used to hang from Brother Fergus's belt. And in his right hand, he held a letter.

Prior Solomon,

You have tried my patience long enough.

You must forget any notion of standing for

election for abbot of Saint Wilfred's. If you do

not, I will shout your guilty secret from the

tallest tower of the abbey. Do not think that you can pay me off with gold this time. I have grown weary of that little game. I demand nothing less than that you abandon your claim altogether. If you do not stand down, then the world will know of your shame – yours and your Turtle Dove's.

Brother Benedict

"So if you would be so good as to wait outside Sir Percy …" came the voice of Prior Solomon from the other side of the door.

Tom jumped in alarm. He'd been so absorbed in the letter that he hadn't heard the voices approaching the study along the corridor – and now the lock was turning. He scoured the room frantically with his eyes but the fireplace was small and there was neither cupboard nor chest for him to hide in. As Prior Solomon entered his study with Percy FitzNigel at his heels, Tom slid silently under the bed.

He squeezed up against the wall towards the back, his nose full of spidery dust, praying he wouldn't sneeze and give himself away. He hardly dared to breathe. Surely Prior Solomon could hear his heart, hammering in his chest like a fairground drum. Tom could just see the prior's long brown feet in his leather sandals and Sir Percy's scarlet pointed shoes posturing nearby. He found himself fighting an overwhelming desire to wriggle forward and see what was happening. He wormed cautiously on his stomach. What a strange contrast they made – Prior Solomon, grave and austere in his long black robe, handsome in his way, and the King's Justice, gaudy as a peacock.

"I don't mind telling you, Solomon," drawled Sir Percy, with a familiarity that made the prior wince, "I considered the church myself once but it was the chastity thing that put me off! Couldn't disappoint the ladies now, could I? Lord, if I was abbot of Saint Wilfred's, I'd have the women of Saint Agnes tearing down the abbey gates!"

But Prior Solomon had no wish to detain his guest for a second longer than was necessary to deliver the thick yellow parchment. With an urgent hand under Sir Percy's reluctant elbow, he hustled him from the room, almost crushing the Justice's silken heels in his hurry to be rid of his visitor. As soon as their backs were through the door, Tom wasted no time. He raced to the window, scrambling back over the sill and tumbling down into the long grass below.

"I called to you but you didn't hear!" wheezed Herbert as they sped across the patchy grass.

"Thank heavens he didn't catch me!" gasped Tom in relief as he rolled down the river bank.

Neither boy was aware of the shadowy form that had appeared at the open shutter and was staring hard across the scrubby ground towards the river, an ornamental writing casket clutched in his indignant hands.

Chapter 32

Lengthening Shadows

"*B* *lackmail*?" gasped Herbert.

Tom nodded. "Listen to this! *The world will know your shame – you and your Turtle Dove's.*" He gazed pointedly at Herbert. "Heard that somewhere before?"

Herbert's face was pale. "Of course. It's the signature on the love letters we found," he replied. "*Your Turtle Dove.*"

"Exactly! And there's more too. *I will shout your guilty secret from the tallest tower,*" read Tom. "It's clear. Prior Solomon has a secret lover and Brother Benedict knew about it. And *we* know who that secret lover is!"

Herbert shook his head in disbelief. "Prior Solomon … and Bessie's mother? But Prior Solomon's so cold … so pure … so …"

Tom raised an eyebrow. "Otherworldly?" he suggested. "I know what you mean Herbert, but there's no other interpretation. Brother Benedict was blackmailing Prior

Solomon because he had evidence against him." Tom waved the parchment. "That would explain why Prior Solomon wanted the sacristy key. He was pawning the chalices and plate to pay the old devil off. But the bursar wanted more than gold in the end. He wanted to become abbot!"

Herbert frowned. "I still can't believe it."

"Which part? The love affair? Or the fact that we might have found a suspect with a really good motive for murder?" He looked down at the parchment. "Let's not tell Bessie about this right now," said Tom firmly. "We need to look at the love letters she gave me again – find out if the writing really is Prior Solomon's before we say anything."

"But how on earth can we do that?" frowned Herbert.

"No problem there," said Tom excitedly, without a moment's pause. "We'll pay a visit to the quillery. Brother Ambrose must have taught everybody in the monastery to write, including our lovesick prior. But we must hurry. We said we'd meet Ed outside Ethelwig's room and the sun's almost over the tower."

In her chamber up at Tirley Grange, Alice Miller knelt by her clothes chest and lifted the lid. She hummed as she gathered the withered sprigs of herbs from between her garments and replaced them with sweet lavender. She paused, her brow creased in a tiny frown. A trail of sea green silk snaked up from beneath a clean woollen shift. But she always kept her fine things at the bottom of the chest, under her workaday clothing. "*Someone's been going through my garments!*" she thought, blood rushing to her cheeks. She twisted round suddenly as the door opened behind her.

"I'm sorry, my love," smiled Gabriel Miller, peering around the frame at his wife. "Did I startle you?"

Brother Ambrose thrust the firebird feathers into the bubbling rainwater to soften the shafts. Then with a practised hand, he whipped the golden quills from the seething pot one by one and cut an angular slice in the end of each before plunging them into the hot sand on the hearth to harden the nibs.

"Ah, boys, what can I do for you?" he smiled, lifting the cauldron back onto the flames as they closed the door.

"We were hoping you could identify some writing for us," said Tom, trying to sound casual. He was clutching one of the love letters that Bessie had found in her mother's chest. "We … we found a piece of parchment … in a book in the library and we wondered …"

"We wanted to return it to its owner," said Herbert.

Tom waved the letter briefly under Brother Ambrose's nose, hoping he wouldn't need to examine it too closely.

"Oh, that's easy," said the quill master at once. "It's Prior Solomon's. I'd recognise that left-handed script anywhere. Such beautiful writing," he mused dreamily. "He could have made a fine illuminator."

"Well, we won't disturb you any longer, Brother Ambrose," said Tom backing towards the door. "We'll give the parchment back to … er … Prior Solomon as soon as we can."

"Oh, before you go," said the quill master, testing the end of a newly-hardened nib. "I've been a little concerned about young Edmund of late – not his usual cheery self.

Could you ask him to pay a visit to the quillery when he has a moment to spare from his studies?"

Edmund had waited miserably in the Swallows' Nest until the sun was over the tower. Now, as he climbed the winding stairs to Ethelwig's room to meet the boys, his stomach was churning. He glanced over his shoulder, expecting any moment to feel Prior Solomon's hand on his arm. The underside of the stairs spiralled skywards like the inside of a giant seashell, the last flight of steps growing darker, the openings more like arrow loops. Ed groped with his hands on the steep stone steps, keeping to the widest part.

The final ascent to Ethelwig's den was a puzzle of wooden ladders that wound at crazy angles around the bells. He paused at the final landing to tuck his robes into his belt when he heard voices from the room above. *Perhaps Tom's here already,* he thought with a start, scrambling onto the bottom rung and beginning to climb. With a burst of speed, he puffed to the top of the last ladder. The door to the garret room was ajar. He paused outside, about to knock, then froze at the sound of Ethelwig's voice.

"I had to keep him trapped inside until the last minute – in case he escaped and ruined everything," said Ethelwig defensively. "I didn't like doing it, Job – I'm not a killer by nature, but sometimes it's necessary to do things for the greater good – to achieve your ultimate goal so to speak."

Edmund's stomach rose to his mouth as he stepped back from the open door, the shadow of the bell ropes like a hangman's noose, dancing in the torchlight above his head. With trembling legs, he clambered back down the crazy ladders and across the first landing. *Where was Tom?* He peered desolately down into the empty cloisters, almost sobbing with relief as Tom and Herbert suddenly emerged from the quillery and made a dash for the entrance to the tower. Ed sprang from the window, caught up his robes and began to run down the stairs to meet the boys, just as Prior Solomon emerged from the vaulted walkway of the cloisters far below. The prior stood in silence in the shadow of the tower, following Herbert and Tom with his eyes, his face an inscrutable mask.

"Of course we must still question Ethelwig," said Tom firmly, as Herbert puffed reluctantly after him up the twisting staircase to the bell tower. He paused for Herbert to catch up. "The blackmail doesn't prove who the murderer is. It certainly gives Prior Solomon a motive, but we need more evidence than that. Don't forget, Job Pug's still a suspect – and quite apart from that, we promised to meet … Ed!" he gasped, as a thunderbolt of grey came hurtling around the bend in the stairs. "I thought you weren't coming!" panted Edmund. "I can't believe it! You'll never guess …"

Tom put his hand on Ed's shoulder. "Calm down, Ed! Can't guess what?"

"It's him! I heard him say he killed Brother Benedict! I heard him *say* it!"

There was a numb silence. "Poor Mistress Pug," said Herbert.

"No!" hissed Ed, casting a furtive glance behind him up the stairs. "You don't understand. I don't mean Job Pug. I mean *Ethelwig!*"

Chapter 33

A Shadow in the Gloom

The three boys trooped down the winding stairs in stunned silence and out into the shady cloisters. Tom felt sick. He leaned his back against a pillar, his head in hands. He was more upset than he'd thought possible, unfairly angry with Ed for being the bearer of such bad news. "Ethelwig's been very secretive lately but I thought he was working on some new invention," groaned Tom. "This is awful. Not Ethelwig – of all people! Come on, Ed. What else did you hear?"

"Shh!" warned Herbert. "There's somebody …"

"Ah, Edmund!" smiled Brother Ambrose emerging from behind the sparkling fountain. Ed jumped like a hare. "Just the person I was looking for. Don't look so alarmed – you've done nothing wrong. I'd like a brief word with you, that's all. Come along with me."

Ed stared at Tom in dismay. The last thing he wanted was to go off with the quill master right now, but Brother

Ambrose was waiting, his arm extended, a kindly smile on his round pink face.

"Don't worry, Ed," said Tom under his breath. "We'll wait for you in the Swallows' Nest. Be as quick as you can."

Tom paced up and down the Swallows' Nest impatiently, stopping now and then to drum his fingers on the parapet. It was too bad that they'd run into Brother Ambrose at such a critical moment.

"I really am confused now," he said in a tense voice. "Maybe there isn't a link between the murder and the sacristy treasure after all. But don't you see what a ghastly position we're in, Herbert? We'll have to betray Ethelwig to save Eli!"

Herbert looked uncomfortable. "I just can't see Ethelwig as a murderer, whatever Ed says he heard. I mean ... what's his motive?"

Tom pressed the heels of his hands into his eyes. "I don't know, Herbert," he said, shaking his head. "Nothing makes sense. Loyalty to Job Pug, perhaps? Fury about Obadiah's death?" He slapped his hand against the rough stone wall. "Oh come on, Ed! We need to talk to you!"

Brother Ambrose opened the quillery door for Edmund to leave. "Well if ever you need a friendly ear, Edmund, you know where to find me," he said kindly.

"Thank you, Brother Ambrose," said Ed, relieved to escape into the passage at last.

"Angelic child!" murmured Brother Ambrose with an

uneasy sigh, picking up an owl feather quill. "But I'm sure all is not well with that boy, whatever he says to the contrary."

Ed crossed the cloisters anxiously, immersed in his own thoughts. He was worried that Tom would have grown tired of waiting for him in the Swallows' Nest. He turned suddenly at the sound of a footfall. Prior Solomon stepped softly into his path.

"Well, I'm going to find Ed," said Tom squinting impatiently up at the sun. "You never know. We might meet him in the warming room on his way up."

But the warming room was empty. "Maybe he's still in the quillery," suggested Herbert, looking round as if he expected Ed to emerge from behind a wheel of maturing cheese.

Tom crossed to the closed door. "I thought we left this open," he scowled, "and look – there's a letter, nailed to the wood." He tore down the piece of folded parchment with a frown. "It's got my name on it."

Herbert craned his neck. "What does it say?"

Meet me in Ethelwig's room. It's urgent. Edmund

read Tom.

"Ethelwig's room!" exclaimed Herbert. "You mean into the lion's den?" He paused in alarm. "What's the matter, Tom?"

"This note," said Tom in an uneven voice. "There's

something wrong with it. I swear it's not from Ed. It's signed *Edmund,* but when have you ever known Ed call himself by his full name?"

Chapter 34

The Silken Prison

As Tom and Herbert crept stealthily up the cat's cradle of ladders to Ethelwig's den, a cart was trundling heavily into the market square of Saint Agnes Next-the-Sea, piled high with weighty stones; rubble from the mason's yard of assorted shapes and sizes, a few discarded gargoyles and the forlorn remains of a broken angel's wing.

"Take what you like from that pile over there," the stone mason had said indifferently, barely glancing up from the design he was sketching, *"but mind you bring it back when the sport is over."*

The town constable had winked – a malicious gleam in his eye. *"It'll all be over by this time tomorrow,"* he grinned, *"don't you worry."*

Abigail Abrahams's lips moved in silent prayer as she heard the ominous sounds from her prison cell, the scrape of stone on stone and the excited shouts of the townspeople as the cart was unloaded next to the market hall. She crouched in the filthy straw, her eyes fixed on her father's feverish body, counting the seconds between every guttering breath with a gnawing feeling of dread.

Tom could see that the door to Ethelwig's room was ajar even before he reached the topmost rung of the ladder, breathless from the climb in half the usual time. Pausing at the top for Herbert to catch up, he brushed a fat moth from his face, wincing as it fizzed to its death in the flaming torch on the smoke-blackened wall.

Silently, they crept across the landing. Tom was wondering whether to knock, when the door groaned open on its rusty hinges to reveal a scowling Ethelwig, his unruly hair a tangle of twigs and leaves. He held a flat wicker basket in his hands, heaving with hairy caterpillars, their brownish heads waving to and fro as they writhed plumply on a thick bed of mulberry leaves.

"Where's Ed?" demanded Tom, pushing past him and knocking over a sack of broad jagged leaves that spilled in a riot of shiny green onto the wooden floor.

"We had a note, *supposedly* from Edmund, but you can't fool me!" Tom stopped, suddenly noticing Ed, a small bundle of terror sitting on a low bench under the window, his wide eyes unblinking, like a frightened little owl. "What's going on?"

"I could very well ask you the same question!" snapped Ethelwig. "What have you three been up to? I'm minding my own business making silk for my ornithopters and I do not appreciate this invasion of my privacy. I've told *him* it's nothing to do with me," he said, with a toss of his eagle nose towards the corner of the room.

"Told who?" said Tom, spinning round.

Prior Solomon stood in the gloomy shadows, an expression of cold fury on his face.

"P ... Prior Solomon!" gasped Tom.

"And now perhaps you'll tell us what you really want, Prior," said Ethelwig rudely. He was scattering handfuls of deep yellow cocoons, like perfect golden eggs, into a steaming cauldron on the hearth. "You couldn't have come at a worse time. I need to boil these cocoons. I've been feeding the worms with mulberry leaves for weeks. Four thousand caterpillars and the leaves from nine trees for a single pound of silk! And that's barely enough for one pair of ornithopter wings." He stirred the cauldron fussily. "We're at a critical time. I'm not a killer by nature, but if the moths bite through the cocoons and escape alive, the silken threads will be ruined. A cocoon is one long strand of silk. I have to keep the moths trapped inside until the last possible minute and then kill the poor devils before they hatch out. You might call it cruel, but what use are scrappy little threads to me? As God didn't bless me with wings, I am forced to make them myself!"

Ed made a sound like a stuck pig. His large ears glowed scarlet. He glanced across at Tom with a look of dismay. Tom was glaring back at him, an incredulous expression on his face. "I ... I ..." stammered Ed. "I only repeated what I'd heard ..."

"O do forgive me, Ethelwig!" interrupted Prior Solomon sarcastically, his voice a simmering cauldron just below the boil. "I'm sorry to disturb your lesson on silk production but I was under the mistaken impression that this abbey existed for reasons other than your foolish ambitions to fly. Pray let us return to the matter we were discussing before these novices interrupted us. You must take me for a fool, Ethelwig, if you think I haven't guessed what you are up to with these boys, poking and prying into other people's affairs. I've watched them carrying tittle-tattle up and down this tower all day long."

"I have no idea what you are talking about," returned Ethelwig, unruffled. "As I have already told you – I have no knowledge of what these boys have been doing, nor do I have the least interest in your private affairs."

Prior Solomon snorted, dismissing Ethelwig with an impatient wave of his hand. "I will come straight to the point now you are all here," he said in icy tones. "I demand the immediate return of the objects that Brother Thomas stole from my writing casket, or you will all face a punishment of the utmost severity. If you refuse me, I will not hesitate to hand every one of you over to the King's Justice this very afternoon. And I am sure you do not need reminding of the penalty for theft!"

"You'd better do as he says, Tom," mumbled Herbert.

"And you may rest assured," continued the prior, his voice rising, "that the word of Prior Solomon will be believed above the malicious gossip dreamed up by some impudent novices with nothing better to do than rifle through other people's belongings. And as for you Brother Ethelwig," he thundered on. "You will consign any lies they have told you to the midden heap of your memory, unless, that is, you would prefer to face a charge of witchcraft before these assizes are over. After all," he said with a smile like the blade of a scimitar, "who in this abbey has not seen you flying with the devil into the sunset? Sir Percy FitzNigel would be delighted to oblige us with a bonfire, with you, Brother Ethelwig, as the kindling!"

"I'd probably have more success if I did fly with the devil," said Ethelwig defiantly. "I am obliged to you for the idea. And I'll tell you again – it is impossible to forget something you never knew in the first place – so you are wasting your breath with me."

A flicker of confusion creased the prior's brow. *Maybe Ethelwig hadn't seen the blackmail letter after all. Perhaps he'd been over hasty. And even if the fool had seen the letter, who would believe a mad flying monk over the prior of Saint Wilfred's Abbey? Perhaps a friendlier approach would bear more fruit.*

Prior Solomon attempted a smile – the tight-lipped kind where the muscles twitch, leaving the eyes behind. But Tom was watching him warily, reading every line of his face. *Maybe the prior is not as calm as he appears*, he thought.

"So, if you would be so good, Brother Thomas," said the prior in a lighter tone, "you will break the habit of a lifetime and do as you are told for once. You will fetch the objects in question and we will put this silly act of insolence behind us. We will all wait here until you return. And don't think to try any tricks," he added in a tight voice, "or it will be the worse for your friends."

But Tom made no move to obey. He could hear the blood

thrumming in his ears. He dug his nails into the palms of his hands, fury welling in his heart. *How dare Prior Solomon use people like this – humiliating Fergus before the whole abbey, bullying Ed out of his wits?* He struggled to order his thoughts. *If I give up the letter and the key now, we'll never get to the bottom of all this. And I have a trump card after all. He knows I've read the blackmail letter but he can't think I know who his 'turtle dove' is!* Tom was breathing fast, his heart hammering in his chest. He felt like a skater, as the ice begins to crack. He squared his shoulders, his mind made up at last. *There might be the devil to pay later, but it's now or never!*

"No, Prior Solomon," he said with a sudden flash of defiance. "You can threaten me as much as you like. I will fetch nothing. And if you force me, I will shout what I know from the top of this tower!"

Herbert sucked in his breath. Even Ethelwig stopped fiddling with his cocoons for a moment, his eyes fixed inquiringly on Tom.

Prior Solomon took a step forward, a strangled sound in his throat. Tom took a step back. He swallowed with an effort, but his voice was unflinching. "Brother Fergus was banished from the abbey in disgrace because of you," cried Tom. "You allowed him to take the blame for stealing the sacristy treasure when it was *you* all along. We know the blacksmith made you a key and that you blackmailed Ed into keeping your secret. We have the key to prove it … and the blackmail letter that explains everything!"

Prior Solomon's eyes bulged. His mouth worked frantically like a stranded herring. Tom glowered back, but his stomach was full of snakes, shifting and slithering, coiling around his heart. The prior was trying to speak but the words seemed trapped in his throat.

"Silence!" he thundered at last, spittle flying. "How dare a humble novice presume to sit in judgement on me? You know nothing! Nothing I tell you." He closed his eyes, struggling inwardly, striving to regain his composure. "I am a generous man," he resumed in a trembling voice, "and I will allow you one last chance. You will do as I say, Brother Thomas. You will fetch me the letter and the key."

Tom was shaking inside, but still his nerve held firm. Now for his final card. "We found some love letters in Brother Benedict's desk," he said, amazed at his own audacity. "We know about you and Alice de Lacy. And if you don't clear Brother Fergus's name, we'll tell everyone what we know – and then you will never be abbot of Saint Wilfred's!"

The prior gasped in disbelief. Seconds seemed like minutes as he stared at Tom, his face creased in confusion. His cheek twitched. *How much more did this upstart know?* He clenched his fist. Tom shrank back, bracing himself against the wave of Prior Solomon's anger. The prior's eyes were burning coals of fury. Tom met his fiery gaze without flinching.

This is it, thought Tom, cold sweat trickling down his neck. *What more do I have to lose?* "Did you kill Brother Benedict?" he cried on a rising note. "Did you kill him because he knew about Alice de Lacy?"

Prior Solomon reeled back as if struck by a blow. Tom

watched, white faced, as anger seethed in the prior's eyes, heaving, swelling, gathering strength. A heartbeat of silence. The lull before the storm. And then in a surge of wrath his rage came crashing down, and Tom was struggling for breath, drowning in the churning waters of his bitterness and hate. The prior sprang towards Tom, black gown billowing. Seizing him by the arm, he wrenched it above his head.

"Did you think I would go to the trouble of killing Brother Benedict," he screamed, "only to be frustrated at the last by a gang of prying novices? For I mean to be Abbot of Saint Wilfred's and no one will stand in my way."

Dropping Tom's arm, he leapt to the wall, snatched up a cold torch from its iron sconce and plunged it into Ethelwig's fire. The cauldron wobbled. Water fizzed into the flames below as the dry tallow caught light with a splutter of blazing sparks. He made a rush towards Tom, the burning brand held high.

"Look out!" screamed Ed. Tom staggered backwards his arm across his face, crashing into Herbert who had sprung towards his friend. "God in Heaven, Herbert!" he whispered. "What have I done?"

"Yes, my friends," hissed Prior Solomon, his face aflame in the heat of the flaring torch. "It was *I* who killed Brother Benedict and may he rot in the uttermost pit of hell!"

Chapter 35

Scarlet Fingers

"So you're the culprit, Solomon," said Ethelwig breaking the stunned silence. Tom stared at Ethelwig in astonishment as he continued to stir the cauldron, unruffled by the figure, towering over them all with a flaming brand – like the Angel of Death.

"See where your meddling has brought you?" thundered the prior, jabbing his torch arm towards Tom. "You and Brother Benedict – two of a kind it would seem. And look where his prying led him!"

Tom's mind was racing. *What will he do to us now? Does he mean to kill us too? We all know too much. And yet there are four of us and only one of him. But then again, he has a flaming torch in his hand!*

"How naïve you must be, Brother Thomas," said Prior Solomon in a level voice, all trace of passion gone, "to think that you could put your hand in the fire and escape without burning your fingers. For you have trespassed into places where you had no right to be; uncovered wounds that will never now be healed. But since you are determined to know my story, then know it you shall – but pray do not presume to judge me until you have heard it through to the end."

"Brother Benedict had few friends," said Tom softly. "But there can be no excuse for murdering a man in cold blood."

"Murder?" replied Prior Solomon with quiet ferocity. "You misunderstand, my friend. The devil got no more than he deserved. He received only justice at my hands."

There was silence in the tower room, broken only by the scratchy sound of hundreds of caterpillars tearing at the juicy mulberry leaves with their sharp little jaws as Prior Solomon began to speak, a distant look in his eyes.

"I had barely seen ten summers when I sailed into Saint Agnes Next-the-Sea holding tight to Abbot Theodore's hand, but I had seen slaughter and bloodshed enough to last a lifetime; three thousand Muslims dragged out in chains and massacred before the walls of the city of Acre, my mother and father amongst them. But Allah in his mercy spared my life. I had hidden in an empty water jar when King Richard's soldiers came for us. And it was Abbot Theodore who found me – a starving boy with no shoes on his feet, searching amongst the corpses for the mangled body of his mother. And so it was that I came to Saint Wilfred's Abbey – an orphaned boy, with no knowledge of your strange religion or understanding of your curious foreign tongue.

"Abbot Theodore was like a father to me but he was a

soldier, not a man of God; a knight first, a courtier second and only an abbot when the hunting was good. So I joined the other novices in the cloisters, where I put away the stories of my boyhood and learned instead of a stable, some shepherds and the three wise men."

Prior Solomon paused, eyes narrowed, staring into the middle distance as if searching the past for his memories, starting in surprise as a newly hatched moth brushed his cheek and flew to freedom through the arched window of the tower.

"But Abbot Theodore did not forget the orphan boy," continued the prior, a ghost of a smile on his lips. "Whenever he was home, he would single me out for particular attention, bestow special favours upon me, little knowing that his kindness would heap coals upon my head. For amongst my fellow novices there was one whose eyes were full of envy and whose jealous heart beat only with resentment and with greed. The ill-favoured son of a lowly butcher. His name was Brother Benedict."

Herbert glanced sharply at Tom with an intake of breath, but Tom's eyes were fixed firmly on Prior Solomon, fists clenched, his knuckles white, like bone.

"At first it was simply petty spite," spat the prior, "cheap sport at my expense; a jibe at my curious manner of speech – my clumsy efforts with the pen. But he was dull of wit and I learnt quickly, outstripping him in knowledge as a shoot in the sunlight leaves its neighbour in the shade behind. And so the persecution changed its course. I woke one morning, puzzled that my hands were stained with crimson ink. And then a priceless manuscript was found in the library, defaced with blots of scarlet – discovered by Novice Benedict. A valuable pane of abbey glass was broken. Then the tell-tale shards were found, concealed beneath a piece of linen in *my* writing desk, by Novice Benedict. He snooped, he pried, he listened at keyholes, he watched my every move and as the months grew into years my fear of him turned to revulsion and my revulsion into hate.

"Oh how I hated him! After a time I took my vows: obedience, poverty and chastity, but my prayers were not for the poor or the suffering of the world. Kneeling on the cold stone floor in front of the high altar with my fellow novices, I begged God to take the life of the novice who knelt beside me – Brother Benedict – my tormentor and my enemy."

Tom's mind was in turmoil, caught between feelings of pity and repugnance. But where was Prior Solomon's mercy for Edmund, for Brother Fergus and most of all for Eli Abrahams, chained up in the town gaol about to be tortured to death? Tom's stomach lurched. Eli's only hope of release lay here in this tower. No one else knew the truth.

"I was in my twenty-seventh summer," continued Prior Solomon, "when I fell in love with Alice de Lacy. I had been a monk for many years and still the comfort of Abbot Theodore's soul; tall, strong and some said almost handsome. The abbot had returned from a mission of diplomacy in foreign parts, eager for some hunting with Sir Ranulf de Lacy, his old crusading friend. He arrived at the abbey and sought me out, urging me to dine with him at Micklow Manor – and it was there that I saw her. She played the harp for us and sang. She was just seventeen summer's old and the most beautiful thing I had ever beheld. Chaste monk that I was, I could not contain my joy when I discovered that she loved me too.

"We seized every chance to meet, and when we could not meet, we wrote. I kept the letters safe, hidden in a secret place in the monks' dormitory, or so I thought. But Brother Benedict was crafty. Nothing in the abbey escaped his malice, from the smallest rind of cheese stolen from the kitchens by a hungry novice to the words of passion between two lovers.

"I was walking alone in the cloisters when he confronted me, sliding from behind a pillar like vermin from its hole, brandishing the letters from Alice in his thieving hand. He threatened me with exposure if I did not become his slave, pay him off, aid his rise to higher office than he could ever have attained by his own feeble wit. He knew I had the ear of Abbot Theodore and he would stop at nothing as he clawed his way to power. And I was helpless prey in his talons, for he knew that I was in love with Alice de Lacy beyond all reason. I would have done anything the wretch Benedict demanded of me as long as he did not betray my secret."

Prior Solomon's voice had sunk almost to a whisper. He shuddered, as if in pain. Then with a trembling inward breath, he continued his tale.

"We should have known how it would end – but hindsight is a sluggish friend. We were blinded by love. We lived for snatched moments, stolen hours of joy. And then one day the blow fell. My beloved Alice found she was with child."

Prior Solomon bowed his head, eyes closed, as if the memory was too hard to bear. "Sir Ranulf discovered his daughter's shame but never the name of the father of her child. My beloved Alice refused to betray me, so in his grief and pain, he banished her from Micklow Manor – and so it was that she became Mistress Miller of Tirley Grange. Gabriel Miller had loved her from afar, a lonely widower many years older than she, who ground her father's corn. He asked for her hand in marriage and she took it gratefully, for he had a home to offer and a cloak for her disgrace. And when a baby was born to them – they called her Bessie Miller."

It was only as the cry of anguish was dying away that Tom realised that it was his own. He closed his eyes and there she was, laughing up at him, her black eyes flashing, fixing him with her earnest gaze of entreaty up in The Swallows' Nest – round brown arms stretched high above her head, battling her ebony curls into a ribbon at her neck. Tom's eyes were full of tears. He blinked them away with an impatient shake of his head. Now was not the time for pity. For the prior's eyes were glittering with a feverish light.

"My own heart was broken in two but my Alice was safe. Safe from the pain of scornful glances, the misery of wagging tongues. Or so I prayed. But someone else knew the secret of our child. *'I have the letters, Solomon,'* Benedict would say. *'The wench grows more and more like you each day.'*

"For many years I bought his silence with favours from Abbot Theodore, and thus the humble son a of a butcher rose to be the richest bursar in England. But then he began to demand gold. I stole the sacristy treasure and pawned it to a moneylender in the town, for the bursar's demands were heavy and I was a desperate man. Then as Abbot Theodore lay dying, the wretch struck his final blow. Gold would not buy his forbearance this time. Unless I would relinquish my claim to become Abbot of Saint Wilfred's on Theodore's death, he would shout my secret to the world, expose my shame, dishonour my beloved Alice and disgrace my daughter.

"But this time the devil had gone too far. For it was Abbot Theodore's dying wish that I should succeed him. We were as different as fire and water, unlike as earth and air, but he loved me as a son. If I bowed to Benedict's ultimate demand, the abbot's dying wish would not be fulfilled. If I stood up to him, then he would ruin my reputation and shame my Alice and our child."

Prior Solomon was perspiring now, tell-tale rings of sweat staining his robe. His face was aflame as the dancing torchlight mingled with the rays of the sinking sun.

"And so my tormentor had to die. I had no choice. It was Lammas night and he had returned from the fair, his greedy purse bursting with gold. I was lying in wait for him. I watched him cross to the lioness's cage and turn the key. It was then that I knew God had sent me a sign. He had delivered the fiend into my hands.

"I waited in the shadows until Benedict had entered the cage with the stinking bucket of food, and then I sprang to the gate and twisted the key in the lock. My heart sang as I turned the handle, releasing the lioness from her lair. I laughed as she sprang upon him, tearing my persecutor limb from limb."

Tom closed his eyes, fighting down the memory of the sight of the bloody remains. When he opened them again, Herbert's gaze was on him, desperate, frightened. Tom tried to speak but his mouth was dry. He swallowed an inarticulate sound and tried again. This time his voice was steady, though his pulse was racing still.

"But, Prior Solomon – Abigail Abrahams is your daughter's dearest friend. If you don't tell the truth, her father will be horribly tortured – killed for a murder he did not commit."

But the prior's control was breaking down. "What is the sacrifice of one man for the greater good of the abbey?" he roared, a glint of madness in his eyes. "It is God's will that I should be Abbot of Saint Wilfred's. This monastery is a den of vice," he cried, his voice shrill. "But I will put all things to rights. I will make this abbey great again," he shouted triumphantly. "It is my destiny."

Tom took a step towards the prior, his nerves like the strings of an over-tuned lute. "But how can it be God's will that an innocent man is tortured and killed for something he did not do?"

Prior Solomon shrank back, raising the torch menacingly in his hand.

"Listen, Prior Solomon!" begged Tom. "The assizes are not until tomorrow morning. You can still get away from here – flee this place forever. And when you have gone we will tell the truth – gain Eli Abrahams' release – but we will never divulge why you killed Brother Benedict to a living soul. Your secret will be safe with us."

Tom held his breath, his gaze fixed on the prior's still face. Was there the ghost of a change in his eyes? A spark of hope flickered in Tom's heart. Prior Solomon's eyes moved, slowly scanning the upturned faces of the boys one by one, as if imprinting them on his memory – and then in an instant – in a flare of torchlight and a whirl of crow-black robes – Prior Solomon was gone. A trail of smoke from the flaming brand hung in the unmoving air. As the door slammed shut, they heard the key grate home in the lock.

"No!" yelled Tom, springing to the door with a cry. "Open the door! Please!" He pressed his ear against the warm planks, straining to hear the sound of the prior's receding footsteps, but all was quiet as a tomb. Then all at once he heard a sound that made his blood run cold – the familiar spit and crackle of hungry flames. A thin spiral of smoke snaked under the door. The wood in the belfry was tinder dry after the long hot summer and in minutes their tower prison was ablaze – a pillar of white-hot flame.

Chapter 36

The Green Ointment

"What are you up to, young Bessie?" came a friendly voice from behind her as she sat on an upturned milk pail in the outer court of the abbey. Bessie spun round with a cry of surprise.

"Job Pug! Don't creep up on me like that."

"I've been watching you these last ten minutes. You haven't taken your gaze off that tower," he said with a puzzled smile. "What are you looking for?"

"Oh, nothing really," said Bessie, reddening. She avoided his eyes. Job didn't look like a murderer – with his smooth round face and periwinkle eyes. Yet Bessie still felt alarmed. "I … I have to go, Job…" she stammered.

But Job Pug was squinting up at the sky. It trembled in the heat behind the battlements of the tower. "Well I never!" he exclaimed, rubbing his stubbly chin. "It wouldn't surprise me if the frogs are in for a treat if that black cloud's anything to go by."

Bessie followed his gaze, shading her eyes with her hand, her hat falling back on its ribbons around her neck. "That's strange. The sky was clear a moment ago – and what's the matter with the rooks?" The birds had exploded into the air, squawking and shrieking, flying this way and that in panic as if a hawk had appeared on the horizon. "It's getting bigger," she said as the cloud uncoiled slowly from its dense dark centre, curling outwards in feathery tendrils of paler grey.

"God's blood!" cried Job Pug in wild alarm, pointing frantically at the battlements. "That's no cloud. That's smoke! Fire! Fire!" he screamed. Bessie gazed in horror as the first fingers of flame flickered like flags of greeting from the mullioned windows of the tower.

The air in Ethelwig's room was already unbearably hot, and choking black smoke snaked under the door. The hungry flames lapped at the edges of the oaken frame, licking between the cracks in the planking like fiery tongues, devouring the dry wood, their breath white hot.

"We're trapped," screamed Herbert, flinging the contents of Ethelwig's cauldron at the door. He groaned in despair, as the water trickled uselessly down the red hot planks and evaporated into steam.

"One cauldron's no good for anything," shouted Ethelwig, ducking as a terrified bat swooped squeaking past his ear. He was frantically scurrying around the room tipping precious caterpillars into a sack. "Help Edmund to the window! Deep breaths of fresh air, there's a good boy," he urged, staggering to the opening and gulping for breath. "Fill your lungs!"

Tom raced from wall to wall, craning out of the lancet windows, vainly scanning the outer walls of the tower for any sign of a foothold. "We'll never climb down!" he cried as the burning door bowed inwards, spitting orange sparks like a fire cracker. The flames roared around the gaps, bathing the stone walls with a blood-red light.

The choking smoke was rising to the rafters. "Who said anything about down?" gasped Ethelwig hoarsely. "Follow me, boys!" he commanded, snatching up a phial of bright green liquid from the stone sill and looping the sack of caterpillars around his neck. He sprang to the bottom of a ramshackle ladder, more rusty nails and knotted string than wood. "Quick!" he cried, pulling Edmund behind him. "There's not a moment to lose!"

Edmund began to scramble after Ethelwig, coughing and whimpering as he climbed. Tom had his foot on the lowest rung when he realised Herbert was not behind him. He turned sharply, searching the dense smoke for his friend. "Herbert," he screamed above the roar and crackle of the blazing inferno. "Where are you?"

Herbert was paralysed with fear, rooted to the spot in the centre of the room, his hands over his ears. Tom leapt from the ladder, eyes streaming, back through the swirling fug. "Come on, Herbert. Come *on!*" he choked shoving Herbert from behind towards the ladder. The ravenous flames were nearing the lower rungs. Herbert whimpered as Tom stamped them out with his feet. "Get up there now whilst we still have time," Tom screamed. "What are you waiting for? We'll burn alive!"

News of the fire raged through the abbey precincts, from the dairyman to the baker, from the laundry to the quillery, where Brother Ambrose started up from his sloping desk, knocking over a phial of coloured acid in his haste to rush to the window. The stench of burning rolled on through the cloisters to where Prior Solomon stood, hands folded, at the edge of the sparkling fountain, staring up at the tower that was fast becoming a pillar of fire.

"Prior Solomon! The tower is burning!" yelled a novice, his panic turning to confusion as the prior stared through him, a faraway look in his eyes.

"It is only stones and mortar!" proclaimed Prior Solomon in a stirring voice. "*Abbot* Solomon will build a new tower. It will rise from the ashes to the glory of God. The air will be full of the chip of chisel against stone and the thud of the mason's mallet," he cried, closing his eyes in ecstasy as the bewildered novice stared open-mouthed, and the filthy soot floated down and settled like black petals on their heads.

The evil smoke was bitter black. Terrified bats swooped, squeaking in panic, slapping into their faces, tangling in their hair as the boys scrambled up the ladder. The merciless flames were at their backs as they reached blindly up the uneven rungs that zigzagged into the bat-infested dark, following Ethelwig as he climbed, nimble as a mountain goat.

"Where are we going, Ethelwig?" gasped Tom his lungs on fire, but his voice was drowned out by a monstrous sound as the melting bells tumbled from their wooden scaffold, clanging, jangling – chiming for one last time as they hurtled downwards in a tangle of ropes and molten bronze.

Up, up the splintery ladder they climbed, snagging their robes and piercing their flesh, erupting at last through a hatch to the sky in a confusion of arms and legs. Half blind, bent double, they retched and gagged, gulping oxygen into their scorched throats. But even as they filled their lungs on the flat top of the tower, the flames waved their fiery arms behind them, reaching up from the trap door into the evening sky.

"Now do as I say!" cried Ethelwig, springing towards a lumpy object covered in animal skins. He began to haul on the covers with both hands. "Edmund's with me in the ornithopter! Tom and Herbert will fly together. Thank heavens for Job Pug and his nimble needle," he exclaimed as the tarpaulin slipped off to reveal the wounded flying machine, a little patchy where the rents in the silk had been repaired but with a new set of tail feathers and an eagle's beak on the front. "Job insisted on repairs – and what a good job he made of it!"

Herbert gaped in horror. "But Ethelwig! We can't all fit into …"

"Nor do we have to!" snapped the old monk. "I told you – you and Tom will fly together. I didn't go to the trouble of making silk just for the fun of it! Edmund and I will take the ornithopter and Tom and Herbert will take … *The Phoenix!*" he cried, whipping off a second cover with a hasty flourish.

The boys stared in awe. No scarlet silk here, no bladder

balloons, but a long thin basketwork body more like a dragonfly than a bird, two sets of wings sprouting from the shoulders. And stretched delicately between the fine wooden struts, the lightest covering of deep yellow fabric – silk the colour of clotted cream.

Tom gasped in wonder but Herbert was already backing away, perilously close to the brink of the battlements and the sickening drop to the cloisters below. "N … no Ethelwig," he stammered looking desperately behind him. "If you think I'm going in that thing … you can think again …"

Ethelwig replied with a jerk of his head in the direction of the roaring flames behind. "Well if you've got a better idea, we'd better hear it now!"

Herbert groaned. But Tom's jaw was set. "Come on, you two," he urged. "This is no time for cowards."

"And besides," said Ethelwig. "These sacks are full of black powder. One stray spark will blow the entire tower sky high! So don't stand there goggling like a geese," he cried, extracting the bung from the mysterious jar of green oil with a pop. "Where's your sense of adventure?" He poured a quantity into his cupped hand and began to rub it into his wrists. "Kick off your sandals and rub in the flying ointment – hands, feet and foreheads – vigorously now, never mind the colour. We need every scrap of uplift we can get." He flexed his knobbly hands. "I can feel it working already. My head's expanding! I've a fizzing in my fingers. A tingling in my toes. I feel as light as thistledown!"

Tom stared at the eccentric little monk with green oil on his forehead and his nose on the wrong side of his face.

Herbert moaned softly, his head in his hands. Ed was sobbing quietly. "Come on!" said Tom in a grim voice. "Hold out your hands."

By now the cloister was crowded with horror-struck monks, craning their necks, gazing in anguish at the flames leaping from the belfry windows. In minutes the summer's afternoon had passed from sunshine to darkness as the dense black clouds trailed like a curtain across the sky. The air was filled with animal sounds, the whinnying of horses, the baying of hounds and frightened roaring from the direction of the beast house.

"Water! The river! The fountain! The well!"

The bake-house was deserted, every cauldron and pan snatched up and carried to the well. The dairy was empty, every milking pail and jug flung into the growing mountain of buckets and vessels in the centre of the yard.

"Men! Form a chain from the well!" yelled the blacksmith. "Pass buckets from hand to hand. Don't just stand there … fill the pails …"

But Job Pug stood motionless, tears streaming down his face. "It's no use! It's no use!" he sobbed. "It's the black powder! It will blow the top of the tower to the heavens!"

There was a sudden terrified shriek. Bessie Miller had dropped her pail into the dust and was pointing up to the bristling battlements of the blazing tower. Two great birds were perched on the parapet, one red as blood, the other yellow as the summer sun, beating their silken wings.

"It's a firebird!" cried the blacksmith's boy, his hair frosted with thick grey dust.

"It's a phoenix!" cried the baker.

"It's Ethelwig!" screamed Job Pug, his wet eyes shining with pride. "Three cheers for Ethelwig," he shouted. "Think up! Think eagle! Think elevate!"

Four pairs of naked feet on the scorching battlements; two pairs of wings. Two brass crucibles packed tight with black powder and the fire's hot breath at their heels. But the green oil was flooding through their veins, filling the boys with daring and hope.

"I feel as light as a lark," trilled Ed, heedless of the stifling smoke, his arms around Ethelwig's back.

"I feel as flimsy as a flitter-mouse," laughed Tom adjusting the leather harness around himself and Herbert.

"I feel as weightless as a ... as a ... windhover," cried Herbert, with a surge of new found courage.

"That's the spirit boys," cried Ethelwig, thrusting a flaming taper towards Tom. "Now watch carefully and do exactly as I do. When I tell you – ignite the powder and beat with your arms as if the devil were on your tail! And don't forget what I told you ..."

"NEVER THINK DOWN!" they chorused. *"Think up. Think up. Think ..."*

"Bird of Paradise!" yelled Tom brandishing his flame.

"Golden Eagle!" shouted Herbert.

"Little Owl!" sang Edmund.

"NOW!" screamed Ethelwig, plunging the burning taper into the brass crucible beneath the ornithopter's tail.

"NOW!" screamed Tom above a deafening fizzing and popping as if the bungs from a thousand bottles of elderflower champagne were blowing off at once. A surge of heat. An absence of air, as if the all breath were being sucked from their bodies. A whoosh like the zip of a firecracker. The ornithopters trembled as the boys and Ethelwig began a rhythmic beating of wings, and then in a dazzling bouquet of fiery sparks they shot from the top of the blazing inferno, like thunderbolts spewed from the mouth of hell.

But the joyful cheers of relief that burst from the abbey court were short-lived. For as the ornithopters streaked away into the crimson sky, the tower exploded a heartbeat behind them, erupting in a million fractured pieces, spraying a fiery fountain of blazing masonry into the blackened sky. The outer court erupted in cries of dismay as a hail of shattered wood and stone began to fall, thundering down on the heads below, a crazy barrage of gargoyles and pinnacles, falling like stone rain.

Chapter 37

The Honey Meadow

"I'm an owl, I'm an owl!" cried Edmund as he and Ethelwig shot into the crimson sunset. Below him, the silver serpent of the River Twist was obscured by filthy black smoke. *The Phoenix* was close behind. He could hear Tom shouting orders to Herbert as they lurched and tumbled through the choking black air, from blazing inferno into the surreal dream of a golden summer's evening.

But their ecstasy was fleeting. As the flying-machines rolled and looped, rocked and wobbled they were losing height. "Brace yourself for landing!" cried Ethelwig with renewed flapping as they screamed over the pig sty collecting chunks of thatch as they went. We'll just about make it to the river!"

"Ow! Ouch! Heeeelp!" cried Herbert, frantically batting black bees with his hands. The boys had overshot the river by thirty paces, scattering wicker beehives as they swooped over the honey meadow, before crash landing in a haystack.

"My arm," groaned Tom from underneath Herbert. "Get off me, you great lump. I think it might be broken!"

"Sorry," murmured Herbert, blinking stars from his eyes. "I'll be more careful where I land next time I fall out of the sky!"

"Well, that was a near miss, Edmund," spluttered Ethelwig, floundering up from the depths of the River Twist, a ribbon of slimy weed around his neck. "Are you all intact? I thought we were going to collide with the pigsty roof!" He was treading water, scarlet silk billowing round him like a skirt. A pair of furious swans hissed down from above. "Ed? Where are you?" he called in alarm just as a stream of bubbles burst on the surface, closely followed by Edmund, spouting water like a gargoyle. He shook his head vigorously, spraying rainbow droplets into the evening air.

"You had me worried for a minute!" smiled Ethelwig. "Now where are the other two? That's my smoothest landing ever! Did you enjoy the flight?"

Ed was treading water too, a rapturous look on his face. "Enjoy it?" he said blissfully, as he dashed the river from his shining eyes. "When can we do it again?"

"It's the green oil that did it you know," said Ethelwig, unbuckling Ed's harness. "It's called lifting cream. But listen to me, young Ed. You'd never try to make it yourself, would you? The ingredients are poisonous – hemlock, belladonna, wolfsbane. Belladonna speeds the heart and wolfsbane slows it down. Quite deadly on their own, but mixed together you get a strong pulsating heartbeat. Seemed to do the trick!"

"I'm so glad you're not the murderer, Ethelwig," panted Edmund as he clambered up the bank, "and I'm glad it's not Job Pug either!"

"Me ... and Job Pug?" exploded Ethelwig. "Don't tell me you suspected us!"

"Well you ... you lied ... I mean ... didn't exactly tell the truth ... about being with Job in the inn on the night of the murder," stammered Ed, reddening beneath the green ointment. "We thought you might be covering up for him and then when I heard ..."

Ethelwig snorted. "I most certainly *was* covering up for him," he snapped. "And who can blame me? Job had a better reason than most to kill Brother Benedict. I knew he'd been at the beast house on Lammas night. It was a year to the day since little Obadiah was killed. I wasn't going to have poor Job accused on top of everything else he's had to cope with. It was a blameless lie – one that does no harm and an awful lot of good. Now where can the others have landed?"

"Over there!" cried Ed, pointing towards the honey meadow. Two dishevelled figures were emerging through the smoke, the blazing tower behind them, like a festering wound on the horizon.

Bessie didn't feel the sharp stubble of the newly reaped cornfield as she sped towards the meadow, her dusty skirt bunched in her hand. Her ankles were bleeding, her hair white with ash. "Oh God, let Tom be all right," she prayed, refusing to think what horrors she might find when she reached the river bank.

"Where are you, Tom?" she shrieked, just as he appeared from behind the haystack. She gazed around in relief at the four scruffy figures plastered with green oil. "How come you're all in one piece?" she said.

"Not quite one piece," groaned Tom, clutching his elbow. "My arm is killing me! I think it might be broken."

"It was the green ointment!" cried Edmund ecstatically. "Ethelwig made it. We had to escape from Prior Solomon. You see, he murdered Brother Benedict! Tom made him angry and he told us everything. And then ..." Ed stopped suddenly, his hand to his mouth.

"Prior Solomon?" said Bessie, startled.

There was a silence. Tom shuffled his feet, wishing he was anywhere in the world but here. "Er ... yes," he said, hesitantly, examining his sandals. "We ... we discovered Brother Benedict had been blackmailing Prior Solomon about something. It ... it was the missing link we needed ..." He paused, searching in vain for the right words. He looked up, forcing himself to meet her gaze. Tom had never felt sorrier for anyone in his life.

Bessie looked puzzled. Maybe Tom really had broken his arm. But something in his expression was making her uneasy. "So did you find it then?" she asked edgily. "This missing link?"

Tom shot Herbert a desperate glance. "Heavens," he cried suddenly. "The assizes are tomorrow! Somebody needs to tell the King's Justice that Eli Abrahams is innocent. You'd better fetch your father, Bessie. Ask him to ride to Micklow Manor. Get the news to the King's Justice before it's too late."

But Bessie was not so easily fooled. "That's all very well," she said in a wounded voice. "But I still don't know the full story. What's all this about Prior Solomon? I've been in this thing from the start, you know. So why do I get the feeling you're trying to shut me out? Does everyone here know something I don't know?"

Chapter 38

The Open Cage

"I'll gallop to Micklow Manor right away," grunted Gabriel Miller, as he struggled into his riding boots in the kitchen of Tirley Grange. "I have to tell what I know before the assizes tomorrow. I must say, I never believed Eli Abrahams was capable of murder, but this news has caught me quite by surprise." He glanced uneasily at Alice. "I'll be back as soon as I can, my love," he added, "but then I must ride to the abbey to see if I can lend a hand. Heaven knows how they'll put out a fire like that with buckets and pails, God help them. They might as well spit on it!"

Alice Miller flinched as the door banged shut and the echo of her husband's boots died away. The shadowy evening kitchen was hot and uncomfortable. Bessie Miller stared at the floor, her face as pale as the puddle of spilt milk at her mother's feet. Shards of a broken jug lay scattered, like jagged islands in a creamy sea, where Alice had dropped it in alarm at Bessie's startling news.

"I'd better fetch a cloth," said Alice in a strained voice. "What slippery fingers I have today. I don't know what came over me. It was such a shock, you know, about the fire at the abbey and … and only to think that you were there, Bessie. Just look at you. Are you sure you're not badly hurt? And what curious tidings you brought!" She smiled faintly. "Of course, I am happy for Abbi, my dear, but it's all so hard to take in." Her voice was uneven, her breath too quick and catching in her throat.

Bessie watched her mother as she bent clumsily to scoop up the broken fragments of pottery. Her throat was burning, as if the devil himself had his hands around it, squeezing out the breath. She ought to offer to help her mother but somehow she couldn't move. She felt as though her life was falling apart; old certainties unravelling like frayed silk. A terrible secret was out. Bessie closed her eyes as the tears began to roll unchecked. *Poor Father! How will he live with the pain of knowing I am not his daughter and that Mother loves another man and that man, a murderer! My God,"* she thought, the room beginning to sway and the bile rising in her throat. *"Perhaps Mother knew the truth about the murder all along!"*

"Ouch! I've goose-fat fingers today," exclaimed Alice breaking the silence. She slumped back on her heels on the earth floor, staring at the ribbon of blood that was trickling down her wrist from where she'd caught her hand on a jagged piece of pot.

"Mother! You're hurt!" cried Bessie suddenly. She sprang instinctively to the floor and began to dab at the wound with the hem of her dress. Alice looked up at Bessie, tears in her pale blue eyes, her face tense, uncertain, like a fearful child.

"Bessie," she sobbed, bursting into tears. "I've wanted to tell you before now. I can't keep the secret to myself any longer. I've tried to summon up courage – oh so many times in the past and somehow … somehow I haven't had the strength … although sometimes I've half-wondered if you knew," she faltered, burying her face in her hands as her whole body began to shake.

Bessie shrank back, dropping her dusty skirt, now stained with her mother's blood. Her expression was cold. She hated to see Alice cry but all she could think of was her father's kind wise face, brown as walnut juice, his hair white with flour from the mill. Her mother had deceived him. And now Bessie had to speak out.

"I know your secret, Mother!" she blurted, her pain giving way to a storm of anger. "Tom told me. Prior Solomon is my real father! How could you do this," she wept, "when Father loves you so much? It will break his heart."

Alice Miller shook her head quickly. The wretched look of a moment ago had gone and now her eyes burned with indignation. "No!" cried Alice. "You've got it wrong. The truth is not as you suppose. Gabriel and I have never had secrets from one another. I admit it," she continued more softly. "Prior Solomon is your father but that was over long ago. I was with child when Gabriel married me and he knew it. When your grandfather banished me from Micklow Manor, dear Gabriel took me in. He loved me in spite of what I'd done. And when you were born, he loved you as his own flesh. Gabriel Miller is your father in the truest sense of the word, my dear. It is not a question of blood Bessie, but of love … and Gabriel loves you … with all his soul."

Bessie gazed at Alice, her eyes deep pools of dread. Maybe her mother spoke the truth but there was still one question she had to ask. "Did you … did you know all along that Prior Solomon murdered Brother Benedict?" she asked in a small voice.

Alice Miller caught her breath, her hand to her throat. "I swear by heaven that I knew nothing of his hand in the murder until you broke the news to us just now. Think what you will of me, but I beg you, do not suspect me of that. My love for Solomon died long ago, I promise you. He became bitter, his mind twisted by the lonely life he has endured. But he has suffered too, Bessie. Brother Benedict knew of our secret. We have all paid a cruel price for that devil's silence – for he was threatening us all, including your father. Gabriel has ground the abbey corn for nothing ever since that evil creature became bursar of Saint Wilfred's – part of the price of his forbearance. God forgive me Bessie, but the night I heard that our tormentor was dead, my heart sang like a captive bird that had woken from a nightmare to find the cage door open."

Bessie stared at her mother as she knelt on the hard ground, a broken jug in her bleeding hands, tears streaming down her beautiful face. She couldn't speak for the choking feeling in her throat but the storm clouds were clearing. She could see the rays of sunlight peeping through at last.

The candles were ablaze in the upper parlour of Micklow

Manor as Sir Percy FitzNigel reclined sleepily on a day bed in the mullioned window overlooking the moat. He was in good humour, his belly full of spiced pork pudding, a goblet of French wine at his elbow and the heady scent of damask roses wafting up from the garden below. Fustian crouched at a high desk, head bent over a mess of scribbles, sucking the frayed end of his starling quill, his cross-gartered stockings sagging around his scraggy ankles like surplus skin.

"What are you waiting for, Fustian?" drawled Sir Percy, puckering his lips around a succulent golden plum and sending the juice squirting into Fustian's eye. "Continue reading the list for the assizes, there's a good man. I want to get tomorrow's business wrapped up before Sir Ranulf arrives back from the abbey. I really can't see why he rushed off like that – it's only a fire for heaven's sake! Of course, I would have been the first to lend a hand myself if it hadn't been for my … ahem … injury," he said, patting his buttock fondly. "Remind me to ride over after the assizes tomorrow and give my commiserations to Prior Solomon." He reached impatiently for the goblet of wine, taking a long, lingering swig. "Now I do hope Sir Ranulf won't loiter too long at the abbey. I've promised to whip the breeches off him at chess again this evening!"

"I thought he beat you last night," mumbled Fustian, wiping plum juice from his eye with a threadbare rag.

"What was that?" choked Sir Percy.

"I said, *I've no doubt you're right*!" said Fustian, shrinking into his robe like a tortoise into its shell.

Sir Percy scowled. He should really rid himself of Fustian

on his return to London, but then a penny a day was so temptingly cheap …

"Pray proceed with the list, Fustian. Surely there's something juicier on the agenda than a few wandering hogs and some stolen firewood. Any deer killed unlawfully – you know the sort of thing – something we can remove the culprit's eyes for?"

"Afraid not, Sir Percy. That's the lot apart from Seth the swineherd – caught using the common spring as a latrine after a night of heavy drinking. Not the most elegant behaviour, but hardly a blinding offence."

"The lot?" exploded Sir Percy indignantly. "Give me the list," he cried, springing up and snatching it from Fustian's desk. He glared at it maliciously. "No wife beating? No hunting on the Sabbath? What's the matter with these people? For heaven's sake, Fustian – the most serious crime here is taking a stranded porpoise from the beach!"

"I think you are forgetting the trifling matter of the murder at the abbey," grunted Fustian, scuttling over to retrieve his list from under a bench where his master had flung it in disgust. "I'd have thought a pressing to death would satisfy even you, Sir Percy," he said with a shudder.

Sir Percy's cruel eyes glinted in the candle light as he reached for a lute and began to twang it discordantly. "I had certainly not forgotten, I can assure you. We must make the most of small mercies while we may, Fustian. The Pope has banned trial by ordeal. Who knows? He'll be banning torture before we know it!" His eyes lit up at the sound of a jingling harness and the whinny of a horse beneath the window. "Fetch the chessmen you lazy louse!"

he exclaimed in delight. "Sir Ranulf has returned already!" He flung open the casement, poking his eel-like neck impertinently over the sill with a familiar bray. "Prepared for a sound thrashing, Ranulf?" he cried, his expression of joy fading to disappointment as he stared down into the upturned face of Gabriel Miller.

"Prior Solomon?" spluttered Sir Percy, knocking the ivory chessmen in all directions with a flail of his indignant wrist. "Ridiculous! We already know who the culprit is. The Jew is in the town jail as we speak. Who is spreading this preposterous rumour? Speak up man!"

Gabriel Miller gazed at Sir Percy in distaste. He was an arrogant young fool but then he had not been sorry to find Sir Ranulf away from home.

"It is no rumour, Sir Percy," replied Gabriel grimly. "He has confessed to it so I am told and ... and it is worse than that. I met the constable on the road. There's a hue and cry out for the prior already. I'm afraid it seems the bird has flown."

For a moment Sir Percy stared at the miller blankly as if unable to understand the simple words, and then his face erupted in a riot of emotions. He'd been cheated – robbed of his sport by that pompous prior with a mouth like a squeezed lemon. Fustian looked away, trying to keep his lips from curling upwards into a smile of delight.

"You must forgive my master," apologised Fustian in mock humility. "He is lost for words. He has a high regard for Prior Solomon. What was it you said to me, Sir Percy?" he asked, his mischievous smirk blossoming into the broadest of grins. "As alike as two grains on one stalk?"

Sir Percy's eyes popped. A dark flush of anger mottled his neck. He rounded on Fustian, eyes blazing.

"What did you say, Fustian?" he roared, his lips peeled back in a horsy pucker of contempt. "You impudent churl! I said nothing of the sort. I never trusted Prior Solomon as far as you could heave a Yule log. I always said the villain's eyes were too close together!"

Part Three

The Wheel of the Year

Chapter 39

Numerology

Tom and Bessie stared up at the blackened tower, eyes half closed against the intense glare of the sun.

"It's still smouldering and it's been two days since the fire," said Bessie in a subdued tone. "I still can't believe what's happened."

Tom didn't know how to reply. It was the first time he'd seen Bessie since he'd broken the news to her in the honey meadow and so far she hadn't said a word about her mother and Prior Solomon.

"My arm's still agony and it's been two days since I broke it," he said quickly, to cover his embarrassment. "I wish Brother Silas hadn't called in the bonesetter. She's bigger than the blacksmith. I thought she was going to tear my arm off!"

"It could have been worse," said Bessie quietly. "You might have broken your neck."

"Well, I've got to call into the infirmary for some poppy

syrup," said Tom. "You should see Brother Silas these days. There are so many wounded – burns, broken limbs, head injuries. I've never seen him so happy!"

"Well, don't forget to ask about Eli whilst you're there," said Bessie. "Let me know if there's any change. I wish Abbi would let me take turns to sit with him. I need something to do to keep my mind off my own troubles."

Tom couldn't look at Bessie, but he sensed she was looking at him. "It's all right, Tom," she said, squeezing his good arm. "I know you feel bad about what you had to tell me. But it's not your fault and I don't blame you. If I had to hear the news from somebody, I'm glad it was you. I've got some hard thinking to do, that's all. It was such a dreadful shock. And to think my real father murdered someone – it's … it's hard to take in."

Tom wished he could think of something to comfort her. Rumours about Prior Solomon were flying like wayward bats. He'd been seen in the woods, in the town, at the crossroads. Only one thing was certain. He'd disappeared like a puff of smoke – and for Bessie's sake, Tom was glad. "I must go, Bessie," he said as they approached the infirmary passage. "Don't worry about Eli. I'll find out how he is from Brother Silas and let you know."

Tom stepped gingerly through the walking wounded who limped in and out of the pharmacy clutching bottles and bandages, shielding his injured arm. He found Brother Silas squinting at a wheel chart nailed to the wall, examining the signs of the zodiac, the Caladrius perched on his arm.

"Twenty-six divided by two," he muttered to himself

tracing a column of figures with his finger. "Ah, Brother Thomas! Just in time for some numerology. These are the numbers of the name Eli – 5, 12 and 9. Add them together and divide by the date on which illness set in. Some numbers are governed by life and others by death – a simple device for predicting recovery. It's a kind of numerical Caladrius if you like" he said. "You get the same result but without the terrible squawking. So 26 divided by 2 is …?"

"Thirteen," said Tom uneasily.

"Oh dear," sighed Silas, stroking Jezebel's snowy back with the tips of his fingers. "Most unlucky for Eli Abrahams."

Eli Abrahams opened his eyes and stared weakly at the dappled pattern of leaves on the whitewashed walls of the small infirmary room. He must have been asleep for some time. The shadow of the juniper tree in the courtyard outside had crept from one side of the open shutter to the other. A few faint sounds disturbed the stillness; the pleasant rustle of the breeze, the comforting coo of the wood pigeons and the rhythmic clicking from the opposite bed, where an elderly monk sat propped on a bolster, knitting a woollen stocking.

Abigail reached out to touch her father's forehead. "You feel much cooler now – you had us all worried for a while. It must be thanks to Brother Silas's tonic: ground unicorn horn and three spoonfuls of dragon's water," she murmured doubtfully. "I'm sure that's what he said."

The door clattered open to reveal Brother Silas looking glum. Tom slipped in behind unnoticed as Silas stalked over to the bed, arranging his features into an expression of gloom.

"I am sorry," he began mournfully. "I've done the calculations and ..." He stepped back in surprise. "Oh! Whatever's this? Sitting up in bed? But surely," he said looking accusingly at Tom. "Twenty-six divided by two is thirteen!"

"Father's feeling much better," said Abigail. "We're very grateful, Brother Silas. I don't think we ever thought we'd receive charity from the monastery, you know, after everything that happened before. We can't thank you enough."

A pink flush rose from Brother Silas's neck to his sunken cheeks. *"I don't believe it,"* thought Tom with a secret smile. *"Brother Silas is actually blushing!"*

Chapter 40

Four Pence a Day

It was late afternoon and Sir Percy FitzNigel's horse pawed impatiently at the dry dust outside Micklow Manor. She was eager to be off, now that her panniers were packed and her disgruntled master mounted in the saddle. The assizes of the previous day had finished almost before they had begun with nothing more than a flogging for defiling the water supply.

"Where's Fustian and his old nag?" barked Sir Percy at a stable boy who was holding the reins of his horse. "I want to reach *The Pious Pilgrim Inn* before nightfall. I don't pay a penny a day to be kept waiting," he snapped. His eyes widened in surprise as Fustian emerged from the door of Micklow Manor wearing a mantle of green cloth on his back, a cap of white silk on his head and an insolent expression on his face.

"I'm here, Sir Percy," he said smiling complacently, his shoulders back, "but I won't be coming with you to

London, I fear. Sir Ranulf is in need of a clerk and has kindly offered me the post … which I have accepted with great pleasure at the salary of … four pence a day!"

Sir Ranulf appeared at Fustian's elbow clad in thick hunting hose, his riding crop clutched in his hand. He smiled mischievously. "I do hope you don't mind, Sir Percy. You never did have a good word to say about this browbeaten fellow. For my part I shall be glad of his services. He writes as fine a hand with the quill pen as ever I saw – and he can even give me a run for my money at chess!"

Sir Percy blinked, his mouth opening and closing like a man with only half his wits. "I … I … I …" he spluttered, spraying spittle into the eye of the stable boy. "You are making a very grave mistake, Sir Ranulf," he blustered. "But don't think you can send him back to me once you discover what a wretched piece of dog's droppings he is! The truth is … I was planning to give him notice just as soon as we arrived in London," he stormed, as his horse tossed its head and wheeled about, almost unseating Sir Percy in its impatience to be gone.

"So it seems it's just as well," called Fustian merrily over the noise of jangling horse brass.

"What was that, Fustian?" roared Sir Percy, his face twitching with incandescent rage.

"I think he said *'May you rot in hell'*," laughed Sir Ranulf, placing his arm around Fustian's narrow shoulders and steering his smiling clerk back through the doorway of his new home.

Chapter 41

The Outgoing Tide

I t is dusk. The quayside of Saint Agnes is deserted,
except for the seabirds mewling and crying in the
mess of masts and rigging, skimming the wavelets,
speeding homewards to their twilight roosts. The timbers
of The Rose of Damascus groan in protest as the last dull
bale of English wool thumps apologetically into the hold
below deck, as if ashamed of itself and its even dowdier
companions, wheat and tin – a poor exchange for quinces
and oranges, marble chips and precious gems.

The night sky is cloudless, the moon, a silver penny on
the surface of the rippling sea. The evening breeze whips
the waves into foamy crests as the mooring lines are slung
to the shore and the prow of the ship begins to rear and
plunge to the rhythm of the plashing oars, away from the
mouth of the estuary with its sweet decaying smell of rotten
fish and into the salty zing of the fresher ocean air. The
Captain narrows his eyes, staring beyond the receding

shoreline towards the silhouette of the ruined abbey tower, which points like a wounded finger into the moonlit sky. He is sorry for the monks and their troubles but the tide waits for no man and The Rose of Damascus has business in Flanders.

He turns with a shrug of his muscular shoulders and strides across the freshly scrubbed planks, mounting a ladder to the upper deck. He is intent on his task, adjusting the main sail that cracks like a whip in the rising wind. He is too busy to notice the strange form in merchant's dress that emerges from the shadows and takes its place in the high prow, like a tall, graceful figurehead. If the Captain had cared to look, he might have wondered at the smooth crescent of shaved skin on the crown of his passenger's head – the merest hint of an elegant tonsure. But not being a woman of Saint Agnes Next-the-Sea, he might have overlooked the fact that the merchant's nose was a little too long to be called handsome.

The Autumn Equinox –
September 21st 1220

Epilogue

The Corn Maiden

It was the Autumn Equinox and the wheel of the year was turning. There was a nip in the early morning air as Bessie Miller flung back the shutters of her room in Tirley Grange. It had rained in the night and the smell of the soft earth was strong. The golden leaves of the chestnut tree were dripping with conkers and rain, and the pink leaved blackthorn hung heavy with sloes.

"Now withers the rose, and the lily is spent, though both once bore the sweetest scent ..." sang Bessie's mother from the kitchen below as the tantalising smell of fresh baked bread crept up between the cracks in the floorboards.

Bessie turned from the window with a sleepy yawn, smiling at the sight of her sea-green gown draped over the clothes chest in the corner. Tonight at the Harvest Feast she would wear scarlet silk with damask roses in her black hair. Everyone would be there. She would dance in the flickering light of hundreds of candles in the great barn under the rafters hung thickly with vine leaves and grapes, her mother's harvest loaf in pride of place amongst the mounds of russet apples and knobbly vegetables. But for this morning her gown must be green; green for the spirits of the underworld, green for the solemn *Blessing of the First Furrow.*

The heavy wheeled plough stood at the top of the fallow field, decked out with coloured ribbons for the holiday, the last sheaf of summer corn balanced on the top and garlanded with flowers. Everyone had gathered for the blessing: Sir Ranulf de Lacy and his spruce new clerk, merchants and traders from the town, shepherds and swineherds from the fields, monks and novices from the monastery – for the memory of years of famine was never far from anyone's thoughts. In the distance just across the stubble field, Saint Wilfred's Abbey glowed golden in the sun, its blackened tower a solemn reminder of the troubled summer, fast drawing to its close.

"Carefully up the ladder now," cried Ethelwig from the bottom of an enormous hayrick at the far end of the field, "and wait for a strong gust of wind!" he called to the youngest Pug boy, whose sturdy brown legs mounted the ladder, a yellow silk parachute trailing behind.

"Poor Ethelwig," pouted Tom in mock sorrow, ambling up with Herbert to join Brother Fergus and his choir of trilling trebles.

"He's had his wings clipped – literally!" mumbled Herbert, munching a mutton pasty and tossing a hard crust to Mungo at his heels. "He won't be truly happy until the new tower is finished."

Brother Fergus laughed. He'd returned from his brief exile in London to an uproarious welcome from the novices, with a saddle bag of the latest ballads for the choir and his mind made up to stand for election as abbot of Saint Wilfred's.

"You're as well equipped as any for the job," said Tom with a grin on the night of his return. "After all, Abbot Theodore couldn't sing a note let alone dance a highland reel!"

Gabriel Miller clapped his hands for silence. He stepped up onto a hay bale, the better to be seen by the people, searching the sea of faces for Alice and Bessie. There they were at the back with Abigail Abrahams, Eli leaning heavily on his daughter's arm. He motioned with his eyes for them to come and join him by the plough.

Bessie's eyes shone as she moved through the press of bodies in her emerald gown, a wreath of corn-ears twined with flowers in her hair. In her hands she clutched the two corn dollies she and Abigail had made in Tirley Grange that fateful afternoon – one in the shape of a bell, the other a horn of plenty.

Brother Fergus stepped forward, his short habit swinging happily around his knees. He raised his voice. "This is a time to give thanks that our bellies will be full this winter, a time to offer back to the earth the fruits that it has given. We will plough the spirit of the corn into the first furrow and so ensure a plentiful harvest next year."

He nodded at Bessie in her Corn Maiden's dress. Taking her cue, she knelt solemnly on the damp ground and placed the horn and the bell in the trough side by side. And then she scooped a handful of black earth, sprinkling it on top of the twisted corn. She straightened up, brushed the dust from her gown and steadying herself on Brother Fergus's outstretched arm, climbed on to the top of the plough. She felt strangely moved as she raised her right hand and drew a solemn circle in the air.

"Blessed be the wheel of the year," she chanted,
"Blessed be the Harvest,
Blessed be the Corn Mother,
Blessed be the Grain God."

Alice Miller, smiling with pride, turned at the touch of a hand on her shoulder. Her expression froze, a deep flush mottling her neck with crimson.

"You have a beautiful daughter, Alice," said Sir Ranulf de Lacy in low tones. "She puts me in mind of her grandmother, God rest her soul."

Alice's hand flew to her face. She swallowed hard. "Bessie is a good girl," she replied in a strained voice. "I know when I am fortunate."

Sir Ranulf inclined his head. "Perhaps you could bring her Micklow Manor one day soon," he said gently, a catch in his voice, "I would be honoured to meet my granddaughter."

The cider is flowing freely now and there will be more at the feast tonight. The ritual is over and Bessie is searching for Tom amongst the revellers. She frowns in frustration, her black brows drawn together in impatience. And then she sees him, deep in conversation with a wool merchant in travelling clothes.

"No, I assure you," the merchant is saying, swinging his tankard of cider to his lips, "there is no wool in greater demand than English fleece. It is the damp climate, you see. The coat grows longer and thicker than anywhere else in the world …"

Tom is nodding gravely. There is so much for him to learn. He glances up, sensing Bessie's eyes on him. She looks so pretty in her green gown with the ring of corn on her head. He winks at her, fingering his broken tooth thoughtfully and then his mouth breaks into a wide smile.

"What would you prefer to be, Bessie?" he calls as she walks towards them across the meadow. "A corn maiden or a shepherdess?"

Bessie throws back her head with a laugh, the wreath of flowers tumbling to the ground. "That depends on you," she calls back merrily. "What would you rather be – a novice or a shepherd?"

The wool merchant is gazing from one to the other, an amused look on his face.

Tom stoops down to retrieve Bessie's head dress from the ground. "How many times do I have to tell you? I have no intention of *ever* becoming a monk," he says with a cheeky grin, planting the wreath of harvest corn firmly back on Bessie's ebony curls.

Another book from CATNIP by Sarah Matthias

THE RIDDLE OF THE POISONED MONK

Charlie's mother is about to be taken for witchcraft, Charlie too. With the aid of Balthazar, his cat, he escapes – only to find himself in another time and a different kind of danger!

In medieval Northumberland there are sinister goings-on at Goslar Abbey. Someone is poisoning the monks. In peril of his own life, can Charlie decipher a runic riddle and solve the mystery?

A fast-paced tale of secrets, potion, hidden treasure!

> "A highly enjoyable whodunnit that will
> keep readers guessing until the very end.
> Starring unlikely hero Charlie, and Balthazar,
> his amusingly sarcastic talking cat, this is
> sure to appeal to inquisitive nine to
> eleven-year-olds everywhere"
> *The Bookseller*

> "I sat up far too late last night reading
> Sarah's book – and I loved it!"
> *Sarah Skinner*, Waterstone's, Norwich

SARAH MATTHIAS

Sarah Matthias is an exciting new author,
with a unique talent for writing gripping
historical mystery stories for children.

Sarah was born in Manchester and grew up in Bingley.
After graduating from Oxford she worked first for the
BBC and then as a barrister. She gave up full-time work
to bring up her children – she has four – and wrote her
first book, *The Riddle of the Poisoned Monk*, to read to
them at bedtime. History is one of her major passions
and she particularly enjoyed researching the recipes and
herbal remedies that appear throughout her books.

Look out for Sarah's next book,
Tom Fletcher and the Three Wise Men.

You can visit her website at www.sarahmatthias.co.uk